LORE

A BIZARRE TALE OF THE DEPRAVITY OF A YOUNG ACADEMIC

by

MARY SMETLEY

This book is a work of fiction. Names, characters, places and incidents are products of the author's imagination or are used fictitiously. Any resemblance to actual events or locales or persons living or dead is entirely coincidental.

ISBN: 1484824652
ISBN 13: 978-1484824658

Cover art by Joleene Naylor

Manufactured/Produced in the United States

Dedication

This story is dedicated to my former husband Ned whose personal life and experiences in academia are its inspiration.

CONTENTS

INTRODUCTION

The story that you are about to hear is entirely fictitious. It is based mostly on the conversations of a fictional character, whom we shall call Lorenzostein, and his psychiatrist, Dr. Perk. Lorenzostein believes that he is not descended from the apes, but, instead, that he has come to us from outer space. Furthermore, Lorenzostein believes that he is The Large-Penised Male. Dr. Perk believes that Lorenzostein is totally psychotic. Furthermore, Perk believes that Lorenzostein's preoccupation with his penis and what he does with it (or constantly thinks about doing with it), particularly with respect to females between approximately 19 and 55 years-of-age, indicates that he is an obsessional sexual predator against whom society must be shielded and protected. Lorenzostein's additional scatalogical preoccupations also indicate to Perk that his mutterings and behavior are the product of infantile fixations and a mind that is warped far beyond the possibilities of repair. Recent research, with which Perk is intimately familiar, clearly shows that mental structures like Lorenzostein's are not the products of developmental stages missed due to the unfortunate vagaries of life. Rather, they are genetically-determined defective asocial personalities embedded in bodies that must be subordinated, contained and triumphed over by the intellectual, moral and spiritual guardians of society -- by natural leaders like Perk and others who have achieved positions of authority and influence.

Again, this story and all of the characters that it contains are make believe. It is presented to the reader solely for the purpose of illustrating the depravity of some of those who live among us. It is hoped that the readers of this missive, as members of society, will be moved to action and will place limits on the heinous acts of these deviant individuals -- for the fuller benefit of harmonious social intercourse among all persons.

Our story begins with a brief review of what we actually know of Lorenzostein's creation and how he first came to believe that he was The Large-Penised Male. What then follows is the story of Lorenzostein's insertion into society and the many conflicts engendered by the clash between his deviant personality and traditional social norms -- as embodied in various authority figures and other bulkwards of society encountered by Lorenzostein in his excursion through life. These issues are then played out more fully in the final chapters.

In relating this sad story to you, we must emphasize and re-emphasize the fact that the characters and places put before you, the reader, are entirely fictitious and in no way do they represent real persons and places. Life is frequently more bizarre than art, so that some among you may believe that you see parallels here with people and places whom, and that, are known to you from your experiences. However, the delusional and totally psychotic depravity uncovered here by the estimable Dr. Perk in the person of Lorenzostein is far beyond the normal range of human behavioral variation. Lorenzostein, his belief that he is The Large-Penised Male, and his psychotically distorted view of people and of social process are concocted fantasy, and have no relevance whatsoever in addressing salient aspects of our social reality. Perk, himself, is certain of this! Nevertheless, despite Perk's unquestioned erudition, it is ultimately the responsibility of you, the reader, to carefully weigh the evidence of Lorenzostein's claims about persons and events and the counter claims of his many detractors.

Let us now proceed with the substance of this bizarre tale.

CHAPTER 1 THE CREATION OF LORENZOSTEIN

It is now generally believed by those who have studied this matter carefully that Lorenzostein probably did descend from the heavens like a meteor and that this took place somewhere near the island of Ceylon, perhaps near the western coast. All evidence points in this direction, and our analysis shall follow a strictly empirical approach uninfluenced by passion or by dogma. What is certain is that the youth, who was called Lorenzostein, who later concluded that he is The Large-Penised Male, appeared at sea somewhere near the western coast of Ceylon. How he actually got there has not been empirically determined, although there were some reports that he descended like a meteor. But, what an appearance it was! There had been bright flashes in the sky, although the day was clear, but there were no witnesses or photographs of his descent. What was recorded, however, were the testimonies of the young maidens who first saw him and who quickly took him in among them.

The empirical evidence upon which we draw for this first appearance, or coming, of The Large-Penised Male is this sample of testimonies taken from the maidens. The sample of maidens whose testimonies we recorded were carefully stratified in the following manner: by age; by their physical position on the beach at the time of the first sighting; by their social status within the virginal society to which the maidens belonged; and by the estimation, by each maiden, of the number of times that she had ultimately copulated with Lorenzostein. It was extremely important that we not procure a sample of predominantly high, or low, copulators, as this may have biased their first estimation of what was to later become Lorenzostein's most noticeable feature.

Two empirical facts emerge from this stratified sample of testimonies. First, the youth, who was approximately 18 years of age, was initially noticed floating at a distance of approximately 200 metres off-shore, apparently on his back. The second, and more rivetingly established, fact was that he had what was uniformly described as a mast, at least two yards, or metres, in length, ascending from approximately the middle of the ventral portion of his body. More riveting still was the uniform observation, later confirmed by closer, hands-on, inspection that this mast was indeed an enormous penis rooted in its proper place in his anatomy and capped by what could only be called a normally shaped tip of gigantic proportions. The youth lay flat upon the water with arms and legs spread apart (as one would if one were to float at sea for a prolonged period of time) topped by this massive post to which was attached, in a very tentative manner as though it were assembled in great haste, a sail made up of a bright green plastic-like material that appeared to be a portion of the vehicle in which he arrived.

Of the above, the stratified sample of maidens was totally assured. What was less certain was what transpired when this sea-borne youth was beached by the currents. It seems clear that his speech and manner showed great confusion. This was obvious, despite the strange language which he spoke. It is also clear that the maidens held his enormous penis in awe as they gently removed its improvised jib while the youth lay exhausted on the sand. What is less clear is the magical powers of attraction the enormous penis seemed to have for the maidens and how this previously vestal group, that had devoted their lives to music and song and the worship of nature and the service of the gods, was transformed by this enormous post-like appendage that seemed to have an existence that was independent from the exhausted, shy and somewhat bewildered youth to which it was attached.

Precise memory of the events which followed seems to have been lost, owing to the ensuing excitement, among our stratified sample. What is clear, however, was that the 32 maidens quickly constructed a scaffolding around the supine youth and his protruding part, and that by squatting on the walkway that straddled the tip and distal portion of his perpetually erect penis they were able to thrust themselves down upon the bulbous end. This gave them great pleasure and produced, from the tip, copious amounts of an aromatic fluid that seemed to be at a considerably elevated temperature and which resembled mud in its consistency. It was also reported, but not in a particularly clear manner, that after a period of perhaps six months in the presence of (or under the influence of) the maidens, the enormous penis apparently condensed and decreased in size to somewhat over 50 inches in length. Although still enormous by most standards, the youth who, when he learned to speak, said that his name was Lorenzostein, was now able to employ his gift without the aid of scaffolding --- much to his own merriment and the more varied pleasures of the maidens. It is with his assumption of more normal dimensions that the youth, through forces unbeknownst to him, felt impelled to venture into the broader world.

CHAPTER 2 LORENZOSTEIN IS INSERTED INTO SOCIETY

Very little indeed is known of the early years of Lorenzostein's life on Earth. One problem seems to be the lack of an appropriate stratified sample to provide a source of data on the subject. However, it is relatively clear that after learning the English language and becoming generally acculturated to human life ways, he traveled, or was transported, to the Pnited Ptates -- to the mid-central portion of the country. There, he was apparently adopted or taken into a family (that of Linnie and Porris), had a younger brother (Cetu), was sent to college, and then chose to go on to graduate school in shitology at a major research institution. Lorenzostein's first academic position was as Assistant Professor of Shitology at U-TRASH, not too far from his adoptive home in the mid-central portion of the country.

We must stress the fact that Lorenzostein viewed himself as a normal Earthling. He only had the barest recollections of his adaptation to life on Earth at the hands of the appreciative maidens -- in terms of both his acquisition of Earthling culture and the physical fine tuning that he underwent to become better adjusted to human social intercourse. After acquiring the basic rudiments of human sexuality from the stratified sample of maidens and their sisters who were not part of the sample, Lorenzostein entered a period of sexual quiescence. He had no realization that he was a probe sent to us from a far off world as a describer, or ethnographer, of the life ways of the dominant earthling social form. Unfortunately, or fortunately, or interestingly, our strange friend was destined to become The Large-Penised Male due to some minor miscalculations by his designers that were beyond fine tuning.

Little, or very little, is known of Lorenzostein's life with Linnie and Porris and Cetu. Apparently, they were members of the Pewish faith, and culturally Lorenzo had this identification, although he did not acquire strong, or any, religious beliefs. He was athletic, but not overly so. He was shy and a bit unassuming during these late adolescent-early adult years. He was a good student, but not mind-boggling in his high school and college academic exploits. He was decent-looking, but not classically handsome by Earthling standards -- tall, slender, gracefully awkward, and strikingly empathetic. In general, he was fairly inconspicuous in these early years -- a rather well-designed social probe. However, Lorenzo did grow a rather full beard in the later years when he was a graduate student in shitology that was similar to those that were commonly worn by students in the 1960s or seen in pictures of soldiers from the Pamerican Civil War. Thus, he began to be separated from other Earthlings and, especially in the 1990s, was viewed as someone who was quite different, although no one actually suspected that he had come to us from outer space.

It is not entirely clear to us at this time whether the growth of the beard was part of his programmed design that was intended to create a provocative social stimulus that had the goal of eliciting a range of human social responses that were of particular research interest to his originators in outer space. Or, whether Lorenzostein freely chose to grow the beard as he began to feel himself differentiating psychosocially from his fellow humans. Perhaps he did this as some form of ritual scarification or similar kind of social identification, as he realized that he was really distinct from other humans, particularly the males, and that perhaps he was actually from somewhere else, possibly from outer space.

The beard was certainly his major visual social marking, along with his hair which, by about age 35, was long on the sides but relatively sparse on top. His enormous penis was actually his most salient visual social marking, but it was usually kept out of sight -- at least in those early years. As noted above, Lorenzostein apparently entered a period of programmed sexual and emotional quiescence during this period of time, as he slowly mastered the Pamerican rendition of human Earthling culture and unknowingly transmitted this information back to the Principal Investigator in outer space through his somewhat shortened, but still enormous, apparatus.

By approximately 36 years-of-age the initial goals of Probe Lorenzostein Earth Dominant Social Form Ethnography (HMN-72-947821) had been achieved, as the Lorenzostein entity had been inserted into the desired domestic and work contexts on Earth. It was at this point that his apparatus was more fully activated and he was impelled along a behavioral path that had been designed to elicit Earthling dominant social form responses to his empathetic personality that was ironically grafted onto a corpus equipped with a penis deemed enormous by human Earthling standards. Furthermore, this gigantic penis virtually had a life of its own (separate from Lorenzostein's mind and empathetic personality), due to unalterable errors in its programming instructions which, unfortunately, or fortunately, or interestingly, set his thoughts and behavior in sometimes unimaginable directions.

CHAPTER 3 LORENZOSTEIN'S MARRIAGE

At 35 years of age Lorenzostein married R and in the course of the following fifteen-years they had five children. They lived in a semi-rural suburb of Trashtown. Lorenzostein taught at U-TRASH, as Assistant Professor of Shitology, and R was also employed in the helping professions as a teacher.

We should devote ourselves to a rather careful discussion of this marriage, for Lorenzostein's mind was greatly shaped by this social context. Furthermore, it was the data generated in this context, concerning his relationship with R and the emergence of his adult social personality as a married human Pamerican in the mid-1970s to 1990s, that was transmitted by his apparatus to the Principal Investigator in outer space. From this sample of ethnographic data, the Principal Investigator endeavored to create a valid picture of the life ways of the dominant social form on Earth. It was for these transmittal needs that Lorenzostein's penis was programmed to be somewhat enlarged. However, several small programming errors in this domain apparently produced a multiplicative effect that was entirely unanticipated.

We must say that R was a very attractive woman -- handsome and refined, rather than sultry and actress-like, although she could have been that too if she had the desire to market herself as such. She was tall, slightly over six feet in height, with very long, straight, dark brown hair that came down below her shoulders in the style of the 1960s. Her face was thin as was her nose, and her eyes were a light brownish grey. Her manner of dress was folksy, also in the style of the late 1960s. Full skirts with button blouses, or sometimes with tee shirts. Or, less frequently, dresses that were simple but attractive, with slightly dipping necklines, although R was not full-breasted. One black dress, with a muted pattern of stemmed red roses, was particularly lovely, and Lorenzostein imagined that when R wore it to work, which she frequently did, that she was seeing her lovers. The mere sight of her going off in the morning in her "party dress," as Lorenzostein called it, was enough to precipitate paroxysms of paranoia in him.

R had many lovely necklaces which Lorenzostein had given to her over the years, but she did not wear them that often, especially as she became older. This irked our hero as they were Christmas presents, or birthday presents, or presents that he had given to R after he had returned from trips abroad or from shitology conferences in interesting places, and he had chosen them with great care. He was pained by the fact that many of these necklaces, which were truly beautiful ethnic pieces, just lay in R's jewelry box, not having been worn for years, while others had been reduced to disassembled beads scattered in her drawer, half-hung on broken strings.

R always wore earrings, and Lorenzostein had also given her some, usually pendulous beads of various ethnic origins. But her taste in earrings seemed to be for things that were quite undistinguished and almost toy-like, and he found it difficult to know what she wanted and even more difficult to purchase what he thought she might wear. In reality, he did not understand her preference in earrings, and it seemed that much of what she wore on her ears were rather simple items which she claimed were gifts from her many female friends and female co-workers.

Lorenzostein often wondered who had actually given these earrings to R, and had the enduring suspicion that they were from her lovers -- either male or female. One particular set bothered him to near distraction. This was a pair of brass heart-shaped earrings that were approximately the size of a large thumb nail. They were somewhat cheap-looking, not an ornament that he would have expected to see bedecking R. Quite out of character, if he actually knew her character at all.

Lorenzostein did not remember from where these earrings had come and exactly when she had begun to wear them. His vague recollection was that he had first observed the heart-shaped earrings when R had worn them for several consecutive days in mid-February, during the fiftieth year of her life. What was noteworthy, actually extremely noteworthy, was that R first wore these earrings, or Lorenzostein first noticed the earrings, the evening that R attended, or said that she was attending, a dinner given by her friend C for several female friends at a lovely country inn on the occasion of C's fiftieth birthday.

At least that was what R said, that the dinner was being paid for by C's mother for her birthday. However, it was not lost on Lorenzostein (due to his highly evolved analytical abilities developed during his many years of study of the complex biosociocultural issues encompassed in shitology) that the party had occurred just after Valentine's Day, and that both the party and the earrings may have had more to do with that festival than with the remembrance of C's day of birth.

Furthermore, or moreover, C had just left her husband of fifteen years and had declared that she was pay. So, R was ostensibly attending a "birthday" dinner for C, her college friend of many years, along with three other women, bedecked with overly-large heart-shaped earrings that had the appearance of symbolic items associated with the exchange of vows. Was this a birthday party for C, or a public (or group) announcement, shortly after their private commitment on Valentine's Day, that R and C were a couple?

Yes, Lorenzostein, with his highly analytical mind that was capable of piecing together disparate and seemingly unrelated items, had cut to the bone and had finally nailed R! She and C were lovers!! Despite the fact that R vehemently denied it, and, furthermore, denied that she was involved with anyone at all, male or female, except for her husband.

But Lorenzostein could see that the evidence, although circumstantial, was overwhelming. The whole business of Valentine's Day, the heart-shaped earrings, and C having just "stepped out" were all-compelling. And furthermore, R had worn both the heart-shaped earrings and the famous black party dress with muted roses. She wore them both not only to C's birthday dinner, but together for three consecutive days -- the complete ensemble -- as though she was attempting to extend some precious moment, engendered during the first wearing, indefinitely into the future. Yes, it was this type of deep social analysis that gave Lorenzostein great pleasure. These mental gymnastics highlighted his ability to illuminate the deviousness of human social life through his uncanny ability to tie together seemingly unrelated threads of life into the complex whole that we are all so anxious to conceal from others as well as from ourselves.

Lorenzostein was also highly suspicious of other occasions on which R chose to wear her heart-shaped earrings. After considerable ethnographic observation and analysis he had concluded that R usually, or frequently, wore the heart-shaped earrings when she was attending social events or conferences at which she would be encountering new men. He believed, or had come to believe, that R had many discreet sexual relationships with men, as well as with women. He felt that the women were mostly close friends, while he believed that her connections with men were both more frequent and more casual, but that they also included a number of long-term relationships.

So, to our somewhat befuddled hero the inappropriate, and somewhat tacky, brass heart-shaped earrings were some sort of signal that R would display when she was attempting to connect with men or women in social situations or, for that matter, on the street. This signal, in Lorenzostein's view, would indicate that this lovely, cheery, schoolmarmy, wifely-looking woman of 50-years of age was "in play." However, her overall demeanor indicated that she could only be approached in a most discreet and respectable manner.

This was Lorenzostein's analysis and it fed his paranoid fears that R, his lovely wife of 22 years was unfaithful to him, and that she would never admit this to him. He believed that it was even possible that she was a pathological liar with multiple personalities in whom the good wifely R personality was not even aware of the devious, libidinous, nymphomaniacal personality. This was a belief to which our poor friend clung until the very end.

We should also comment on R's extremely gracious and cheery demeanor, as this was her most salient social feature and served as an object of Lorenzostein's intense social analysis. Cheery, relentlessly cheery, is what R was! Gracious as well, and at times more than a bit befuddled, but R was nothing if not cheery. Yet, she was not only cheery, she was a sweetipie. A very nice person. Even a saint! For, in addition to being cheery, R was 'good'! She had been raised as a Praker and had been taught since her youth to be a caring and giving person. Caring and giving to the wretched and the poor and to the plentitude of ethnic minorities, if not to her immediate family and her husband Lorenzostein. Furthermore, or moreover, what Lorenzostein wanted R to give him was not exactly within R's ability to give, at least to him, nor part of her definition of 'good'. He suspected that this was something that she was able to give to others when she was embodied in one of her variant personalities, but it was not something accessible to Lorenzostein.

At this stage of our story it is difficult to convey to the reader how R's cheeriness impacted our poor friend and was viewed by him, for the reader does not yet really know, because we have not yet really discussed, much about Lorenzostein's various needs. However, our hero's human personality had developed largely in the context of his marriage to R, and except for the unpredictable effects of some minor programming errors made during his creation, who he was as an Earthling Dominant Social Form had largely been determined by his experiences in working out his psychosexual relationship with R and in raising a family of five children with her.

This being said, we can now state that Lorenzostein was initially drawn in by R's cheeriness, but during the course of his marriage to her (and in the process of explaining to himself and others his increasingly consuming psychosexual needs) our friend had come to see this cheeriness, at least as it was directed toward him, as superficial and highly ritualistic. Yes, ritualistic, rather than deep and authentic, is how he had come to see it, and he was pleased that he was able to apply his professional training in shitology in this analysis of R's behavior, particularly as it related to him.

Lorenzostein had actually come to view R's cheeriness as an extreme form of deviousness. By being so nice, and 'good', and relentlessly cheery, R was putting herself beyond reproach and, more importantly, beyond suspicion! These observations, and the subsequent data derived from them, formed the basis of a thick analysis in his mind; more precisely a thick shitological analysis of this highly textured behavior. Viewed within the context of mid-range theory derived from a melding of the shitological perspective and that put forward by Peertz in his classic 1973 work, Lorenzostein was able to develop a deeply textured assessment of the psycho-social-sexual motivation behind R's cheery onslaught.

First, Lorenzostein was certain that R was

unfaithful to him irrespective of her many denials and in spite the fact that he relentlessly spied on her comings and goings at work and during her rather long lunch periods -- without ever having discovered any indiscretions on her part.

It was during these extended lunch periods, when R moved across town from one worksite to another, that he suspected -- or was certain -- that R was carrying on almost daily encounters with a multitude of male and female lovers.

It had become increasingly clear to him (due to his highly developed analytical abilities honed over the years in writing innumerable scientific papers based on his work in pure shitology as well as his work on multi-disciplinary bioshitological studies that he had carried out at multi-centre cooperating institutions) that R's cheeriness was a calculated offensive strategy designed to deflect suspicion away from her for her many sexual prevarications. Who would ever suspect that this wifely, churchy, 'good', saintly, relentlessly cheery and suffocatingly maternal woman could ever be a hopelessly compulsive bisexual nymphomaniac scurrying from one paramour to another between her many good deeds, her carpooling of her children, her tending of her garden and flowers, and her purposefully contrived ostentatious displays of domesticity in walking her dog Para!

Lorenzostein was particularly certain that these obviously overblown manifestations of domesticity were contrived behaviors designed to deflect his suspicions away from her hidden nymphomaniacal tendencies. Her daily walking of Para, during which time she would cheerily chat with neighbors whom she encountered with or without dogs, was obviously an attempt on R's part to portray her rectitude and domesticity to the social group and consequently to undermine his credibility to the social group if he were ever to find concrete evidence of her wrongdoings and attempt to air them publicly. Who would ever believe the notoriously lusting Lorenzostein's contorted claims about R's nymphomaniacal forays if they were countered by the sincere denials or R, a stellar member of society?

There were other false domesticities as well! Although cheery, R was very reserved with Lorenzostein and discouraged his many physical advances around the house -- his kissing in the kitchen and his patting of her butt, and his insatiable desire, or need, for multiple daily copulations. She deflected these demonstrations of affection and desire and orchestrated an everyday life of cheery distance. Yet, when they would take their occasional walk together around the neighborhood R would invariably take his arm, or put her arm over his shoulder, in an exaggerated public display of what he felt was superficial affection that had the sole purpose of falsely signaling to their friends and neighbors that all was well in this blissful marriage, thus concealing the turmoil, the deviousness, the plotting and planning, and the profound physical and emotional disengagement that characterized their relationship.

CHAPTER 4 THE MIND OF LORENZOSTEIN

We have seen that as an Earth Dominant Social Form Probe, Lorenzostein was programmed to acquire the basic rudiments of Earthling culture and to undergo early personality development so that he could be inserted into human society. However, the Principal Investigator's main research goal was to explore the psychosexual development of a male dominant social form (human) within the marital relationship -- or, more precisely and scientifically, what he called in the research protocol "the adult continuous mating relationship." To this end, prior to his relationship with R, Lorenzostein's overall process of maturation was somewhat stunted, but following marriage, his psychosexual development was programmed to accelerate significantly and data on these developmental events and crises were transmitted to the Principal Investigator in outer space via his enormous antenna.

The Principal Investigator was employing a research strategy devised by him and others which maintained that an in-depth study of the psychosexual development of a representative individual during a complete reproductive cycle (from marriage to the time that the last child leaves the parental household) would provide unique insights into the entire sociocultural milieu of the dominant social form social group. Unfortunately, the Principal Investigator had only a superficial understanding of sampling theory and the limitations of a sample of one. His research strategy had not accounted for the additive, or multiplicative, effects of a number of minor programming errors, particularly those pertaining to the developmental schedule for the growth of Lorenzostein's penis.

As a consequence of these particular factors, the emotional and sexual components of Lorenzostein's rapidly awakening personality were thrown into overdrive, and his emerging needs in these areas initially sought recognition in his marital relationship with R. This unfortunately heightened developmental schedule (which was very much an artifact of the: Principal Investigator's research design; the additive and multiplicative programming errors with respect to the penis; and the peculiarities of R as a wife, or mate in the Principal Investigator's terms) led to the evolution of the social entity that came to be known as The Large-Penised Male and the ensuing legends surrounding his sexual exploits and his perambulations through the social milieu in which he found himself inserted. A careful consideration of these factors will provide us with: important insights into scientific methodology; a greater understanding of the importance of the marital context in psychosexual development; and a fuller appreciation of how minor programming errors affecting penis size and, consequently sexual development, may help account for the more extreme behavioral variation observed among humans, some of whom, like Lorenzostein, may have come to us from outer space.

By now it should be abundantly clear to us that Lorenzostein had a gigantic penis (including the reasons why his apparatus was so large) and that he was married to R, who usually did not wear the nice necklaces that he had given her, but who did occasionally, or frequently, wear the tacky brass heart-shaped earrings that caused him so much concern. What has not yet been revealed to the reader is exactly how Lorenzostein came to be known as The Large-Penised Male, and how a thick and highly textured analysis of his mental make-up can shed considerable light on the incredible events that we are about to convey.

Perhaps the initial thing that we should directly say about Lorenzostein is that at first he truly did not realize that he had a gargantuan penis. What this unsuspecting lad brought with him from the depths of outer space is something that had not been unfurled during the entire course of vertebrate evolutionary history on Earth. Furthermore, this something was doubly remarkable not only for its magnificent length, but for its firm and highly textured (some would say roughened) surface. Although its length and texture were particularly noteworthy, what was even more spectacular, to the unsuspecting observer, was its dark reddish purple color.

Upon first encountering this colossal apparatus in its fully extended attitude, most viewers experienced an initial palpable fear reaction. The composite picture of Lorenzostein's full black beard, his lustful looking bluish-green eyes, his lips which seemed always to be searching for the full feeling of soft female lips, or for the feeling of bulbous nipples in the initial state of arousal, led, in the average viewer, to the sense of being in the presence of something wild and primitive -- of being in the very presence of a 'forest creature'. Visualization of our hero's stupendous thing invariably drove females to paroxysms of uncontrollable desire, a sense of absolute need so profound that life itself seemed unbearable without being visited by its plentitude and by the wild, but somewhat boyishly ingenuous, 'forest creature' to which it was so firmly attached.

Among males there was an entirely different reaction, and this was of great interest to the Principal Investigator. Most males who somehow caught a glimpse of his gigantic apparatus did not see it in its fully unfurled state. Male visualizations of Lorenzostein's penis usually occurred in a public men's room when minimal social information was being transmitted and the apparatus had consequently not achieved its full form that was necessary to transmit data to outer space. However, on several occasions at U-TRASH our friend had entered the men's washroom in the presence of individuals who had particular social valencies to him -- professionally competitive, or hostile to him within the context of the politics of the Department of Shitology, or individuals who were aggressively pomosexual in the refined manner of academia. During these times, while he listened, or was subjected , to the banter of the washroom, the mighty staff unfurled to near full length (in order to transmit this important social data to the Principal Investigator in outer space) as he stood before the urinal. This produced the most amazing sight of Lorenzostein reaching the urinal from half way across the men's room with his enormous reddish purple, highly textured tube capped by what could only be described as the 'cap of caps'. We should also say that Lorenzostein's penis was stout, but not unaesthetically so. Certainly, it did not have the dimensions of a water main. It was perhaps three times the normal thickness, but not too wide to impede its proper pneumatic function.

The reaction of other males to this sight was invariably one of derision, contempt, and disgust. Not one single positive comment, even in a jocular manner. This thing, which would have brought accolades of comradely acclaim to males who were part of the dominant socio-religious group, brought looks of suspicion and contempt toward Lorenzostein, despite what an impartial panel of observers certainly would have concluded was an aesthetically magnificent, and truly wondrous, appendage. It was some of these early washroom encounters which alerted Lorenzostein to the fact that he was somehow different from other humans and that he, with or without his magnificent penis unfurled, elicited markedly different and unpleasant

responses from members of the male sex compared to those that he received from females.

At this point we have, through a very carefully layered descriptive analysis, conveyed a highly textured picture of: Lorenzostein's phenomenal penis; its visual elements; his own perception of the thing; and the flutter it caused in the men's washroom when it was put to its most innocent, and basic, task. However, we have not yet dealt with what our large-penised hero really did with this great thing. To what social uses it was put? And, how this gigantic, programming error-induced mutant penis, with a virtual life of its own, had cut a swath through femalehood and had wrought havoc throughout sedate society.

Having said the above, we may now proceed with a highly textured thick analysis of Lorenzostein's growing obsession with his penis. This obsession was engendered not because he originally thought that his penis was beautiful, or even nice, or even longish. As we have seen, in his early years he really did not think too much about his penis. It was only when he began to bestow it on human femalehood that he began to realize, quite to his ingenuous amazement, that he had something that was highly desired, something that females wanted desperately. Furthermore, the females seemed to sense that he had this highly sought after item without their ever having seen it. By some unknown process they knew that this shy and soft-spoken lad had what they wanted -- an enormous penis that had an autonomous life of its own and which lived far beyond the laws of normal human intercourse. A penis that somehow had become separated from the 'forest creature' to which it had belonged and had become attached to the body of a reasonably attractive, humorous, well-educated, fellow who went by the name of Lorenzostein. By looking into our mild-mannered friend's somewhat wild blue-green eyes, they seem to have been able to see that this highly socially-appropriate-looking body, and its attendant superficial personality, were really the vehicle for a penis of unimaginable length and vitality, and that this relatively reserved penis bearer was truly the much anticipated Large-Penised Male who was prophesied to come for the more complete benefit of all femaledom.

The reader may ask why Lorenzostein only belatedly realized that he was The Large-Penised Male given the obvious fact that soon after his arrival from outer space he was put to such good and incessant use by the maidens on the beach, as reported above by the stratified sample from that group. The reason, as reported above, was that his human personality was only going through its initial phase of development during this early period of adaptation, adjustment, and refitting (up to a point, so to speak) to the Earth dominant social form cultural milieu. He had virtually no recollection of these events, and it was only later, when he entered into the marital relationship with R, and his psychosexual development was accelerated, that he suddenly became aware of the vast arsenal that he carried between his legs.

Perhaps it would be helpful to the reader if we would provide you with greater details, more specifics, about our protagonist's actual relationships with particular women, rather than the vague generalizations based on his statements as they have come to us from Dr. Perk's own analysis following his breakdown. We should report, however, that it was extremely difficult, virtually impossible, to directly interview the women involved. This is because Lorenzostein quite frequently carried out his affairs with married women who, obviously, were unwilling to discuss the matters in a public forum. Furthermore, Lorenzostein, feeling a lack of empathy from other males, had never confided anything about his innumerable and varied sexual exploits to them. What we do know is what he revealed to Perk during the course of the eminent psychiatrist's treatment of him. It is the data from his therapy, supplemented by direct revelations by a limited number of the principal participants, that forms the basis of our continuing discussion, and these data must be treated in the most highly confidential and respectful manner despite their superficially prurient nature.

Lorenzostein sought Perk's assistance when R discovered that he was having a long-term affair with N. Why R married Lorenzostein is unknown. It is also unknown how R did not know that he was having affairs with virtually all of the women in his and her social network, and many outside of it, especially with women with: large breasts; medium sized breasts that were disproportionately large and protuberant, in the European fashion, for their medium to slender bodies; small breasts with long hair, or short hair and attractive faces with soft lips; longish dirty-blond hair; long brown hair; long black hair; frizzy hair; lightly pigmented skin with a flush of red in the cheeks and lips; medium pigmented skin (he really could not say olive because he really had never seen a women with olive-colored skin, and olives have so many different colors that the reader would surely be confused); darkly pigmented skin with large, medium, and small breasts and various types of hair; disproportionately large buttocks affixed to relatively slender, medium, or slightly large frames that were balanced by breasts of ample magnitude.

For whatever reason, R chose to ignore, or not see, (unless it was thrust by circumstances fully in her face so she could not possibly block it out and still claim to be conscious) the fact that women tended to seek Lorenzostein's affections and that her poor husband had absolutely no control when confronted, or fronted, by an aroused woman, slightly intoxicated or sober, who, upon seeing our appealing friend, decided that she must have him within. Of course there were also occasions when unsuspecting women, perhaps even unaroused women (some burdened by the repressive conventions of society, and others, a limited number, somehow unmoved -- perhaps due to hormonal irregularities on their part or their fear of ecstasy), were somehow unmoved by what Lorenzostein was able to bring to bear on the situation. This occasionally led to awkward consequences when they were confronted with our hero's rapid escalations. R dealt with Lorenzostein's need to copulate with virtually all women in sight by totally ignoring everything that took place out of her presence and by totally ignoring everything that took place within her presence. Furthermore, over the years, she attempted to steer their joint social lives away from contexts that contained socially appropriate women of some nubility, for she knew that her rabid husband would generally not initiate liaisons with socially inappropriate women in her presence, although in the depths of her mind she suspected that in the world at large that he would not show such control. Therefore, their social life was somewhat circumscribed, involving a limited number of close friends that Lorenzostein, with commendable restraint, and solely to achieve a modicum of domestic tranquility, had declared off-limits. Actually, a short-term mistress, who he recalled had a butterfly tattoo on her buttocks before such things were popular, had advised him not to "shit on his own doorstep," an admonition that our hero reluctantly embraced.

CHAPTER 5 N

We could say a few words about N, but the reader must respect the fact that what we relate is highly confidential and is derived from Dr. Perk's records which were kept in a locked cabinet without indication of the patient's name, in accordance with U.S. Regulation 69 regarding confidentiality of psychological and psychiatric records. Actually, we cannot be absolutely certain if these records pertain to N, or Lorenzostein's comments about N, since they do not actually have a label identifying them as such -- for the above reasons of complete confidentiality to which Perk adhered scrupulously. However, they do refer to Lorenzostein and to a young woman called N who appears to have been approximately 23 years of age in the late 1970s and 44 years of age in 1998, when the entries cease, following Perk's final breakdown.

There are many scribblings in the margins which appear to be in Perk's hand, but which were written in a darker-colored ink and in a somewhat shaky manner. These seem to be random entries made by Perk at a later date, perhaps when he was reviewing Lorenzostein's file for insurance purposes or as a source of materials for one of the many scholarly papers that he had written. "Tits From Heaven" is a frequent marginal notation usually in dark thick lines that seem to reflect repetitive, possibly even obsessional scribblings that were ringed by pen stab marks suggesting violent tendencies. "Enormous Tits, Bigger Than The Entire Universe" was another frantic, and somewhat overstated, entry. The pages also contained multiple stains, some of which were superimposed on one another. DNA analyses have indicated that these were Perk's semen stains left by what appears to have been incessant masturbation onto these sheets over an extended period of time -- perhaps twenty years.

In addition to these copious, and somewhat sticky, files, along with Perk's composite file on Lorenzostein, information on our hero's relationship with N has been procured from: R's truthful comments while under hypnosis as part of Lorenzostein's treatment; interviews with various unnamed former students who attended U-TRASH while Lorenzostein and N were involved in their torrid and despicable relationship; interviews with JB Hawkblack, Red Grant, Buck Schmuckperson, Vladimir Haverford, Fey Nayward, Shenzi Rafel, and other members of the Department of Shitology at U-TRASH, along with statements made during their dispositions and at their trials.

It is obvious from Perk's files that N was an extremely striking woman. At first, it was uncertain whether Perk had actually seen N. It does not appear that she ever had an individual appointment with him or that she saw the estimable doctor along with Lorenzostein. However, the vivid descriptions of N in Perk's files suggest that Perk had possibly become obsessed with the lurid visions of N conveyed to him by Lorenzostein, and that he had actually observed N, or had engaged in some sort of long-term voyeuristic surveillance of N, and may even had made attempts to gain favor with her in some surreptitious manner. There is no other possible explanation for the apparent intensity of Perk's emotional involvement with N, given that she was merely the mistress of one of his patients.

Based on Perk's records and the various sources listed above, it is clear that N was quite tall, approximately five feet ten inches in height, and that she had brownish blond hair that hung almost to her shoulders. N apparently had a rather dramatic visual impact on men, and observers uniformly commented on three salient aspects of her appearance. First, and foremost, so to speak, were what were universally described as enormous breasts that were so huge, and full, and limpid that they glared from her upper torso like two gigantic high-beamed headlights that riveted the eyes of all that beheld them (male and female alike) in an inescapable grasp. It was reported by many males that on first seeing this splendid sight that their lower jaw dropped in total amazement, followed shortly thereafter by a copious salivary flow and a certain sense of well-being that lasted a lifetime -- as though they had been placed in the presence of one of the principal goddesses of classical times.

In an awkward, groping, and rather begrudging way, Perk made what may have been a most important connection (so to speak). This insight, which is one of many testaments to Perk's analytical expertise, was that N's tremendous breasts were equally as preposterous as was Lorenzostein's signature characteristic, and that they both, N and Lorenzostein, seemed to be placed completely apart from other humans, if only for these reasons. Or, as

Perk mused in one of his early entries when he still seemed clear-headed and detached on the matter, "This torrid and somewhat irrational relationship between N, a young woman with enormous breasts and a wild demeanor, and Lorenzostein, an older professor who apparently has a gigantic penis, represents the classic confrontation between pure femininity and pure masculinity that is frequently portrayed in Preek mythology.

A second visual aspect of N, that was uniformly described as "eyeball melting" by all observers, was the plentitude of N's bottom -- more discreetly referred to as her derriere by some, and more frequently referred to as her ass by others. Yes, N was described as having an extremely feminine and highly attractive bottom that Perk referred to as an 'ass of asses' and as a 'thousand-year ass'. It is also clear from these descriptions that what had caught these observers' eyes was not a shapely, soft, but modest female cushion. No, rather, N's rear portions were not seen as playful little knolls upon which one might wish to lay one's head, but, instead, they were described as enormous sensuous mare-like quarters that, like her frontal aspect, had the effect of completely riveting any eye which had the very good fortune of having this exemplary piece of female anatomy saunter into its field of vision.

The third and, should we say, equally dramatic feature of N was her face. N: had a brilliant mind and was truly a scholar (as an undergraduate in piochemistry, and afterwards in an aspect of jurisprudence); was extremely well-read and was a published novelist; was a highly empathetic person; and was a good mother to her three sons. However, despite these admirable characteristics, N's appearance, or the manner in which she presented herself in everyday life, was dominated by the fact that she had a very attractive and lustful-looking face and mouth, and slightly tired-looking eyes, that, coupled with her two other physical attributes described above, created an image, or a visual impression, of extreme sensuality and utter behavioral abandon that was many times more powerful than the sum of their individual anatomical parts.

In a women with a face with less sheer beauty and obvious character, breasts and a caboose of the size that were fitted onto N may have seemed obscene. Yet, when welded together in the perfection that these elements achieved in N they produced, in the terms employed by one colleague when he first cast his eyes on a slightly inebriated N together with Lorenzostein at a reception at U-TRASH, a veritable 'Viking Goddess'.

N had a unique type of sensuality that would literally bring vehicular traffic to a stop. Before the rise of political correctness in the early 1980s, her presence on a sidewalk would bring trucks and taxis, and most other vehicles, to a screeching and appreciative halt to an extent that was only seen in fictional Italian films with highly stylized sex-symbol actresses. However, N despised this attention and the cheapening sexual label which most men seemed to attach when first encountering her. Nevertheless, N did have an extremely strong sex drive. However, her favors were not distributed randomly or widely, and she formed a limited number of strong emotional-sexual relationships, although her choice of partners, including Lorenzostein, showed a certain lack of measure.

N's tragedy, or one aspect of her tragedy that was quite beyond her control, was that she had such an overwhelmingly erotic impact on men that they were not able to deal with her as a person. A man, any man who was not pay (and even some of them), could not be in her presence and think of anything else except kissing her lips and her full breasts and copulating with her incessantly until the end of time. Just by looking at N was to see the embodiment of possible total sexual and emotional ecstasy. Consequently, most men, especially those who did not have, or never had had, a modicum of sexual and emotional intensity in their lives, were threatened by her. They were unhinged because N personified what they, in the depths of their usually self-centered hearts and overly materialistic minds, wanted but knew they could never have. So, they would reject her as a person, and the unattainable option that her visage presented to them, by cheapening her obvious sensuality, the thing to which they were most attracted.

Thus, in many ways N was a marginalized person, the object of unwanted overtures from the less cultured and restrained segment of the male population, and hostility from among more socially appropriate males who found her too arousing to be near for extended periods of time.

N's intellectual arrogance and her near total disinclination to suffer fools, pedants, and braggarts also did not serve her social cause in the long run.

N was a 23-year-old student in the Department of Shitology, and she and Lorenzostein began their relationship shortly after they met. Like all men, our hero was bedazzled when he first lay his eyes on N as she self-consciously (in those days she knew that wherever she went all male eyes were riveted on her, which made this rather shy and introspective young lady feel extremely aware of her social impact and quite uncomfortable about it) crossed a university plaza fronted and trailed by her signature silhouettes and topped by her Viking visage. He next encountered N chatting with, or being advised, in the office of Vladimir Haverford, one of his colleagues in the Department of Shitology. Lorenzostein later learned from N that Vladimir (who presented himself to the students as an overly sincere faculty member who was excessively solicitous of the undergraduate students, probably in compensation for the fact that he was truly a bit slow mentally and that his scholarship could only be characterized as pedestrian, although quite politically correct) had been pursuing N in a rather indirect and restrained manner, but that he had never gotten himself together to make an unambiguous approach to her.

N enrolled in a class that our hero was teaching and their relationship began shortly thereafter, although N did later remarked to him that she was surprised that he had not asked her out to lunch until two weeks of the semester had passed. Lorenzostein clearly had taken the initiative with N. He had invited her to join him for lunch and shortly thereafter they were in bed and had begun a rather torrid relationship. But when thinking about it retrospectively, in the course of his therapy with Perk, it became increasingly obvious to him that N had chosen him, that she had taken the initiative, that she had decided that he, Lorenzostein, was the one that she wanted. She had put herself in a position, in the class that he was teaching, where he, as a normal male, perhaps an extra-normal male due to his particularly fortunate or unfortunate endowment which we have described above, would respond predictably to her. And she, in this instance because he was the chosen one, would respond to him in a clearly encouraging, but socially appropriate manner.

This was quite a realization for Lorenzostein as he had always thought that it was the male who chooses the female and then doggedly pursues her until consummation. In the process of learning to be a male he had constantly told himself that he must take the initiative, that taking the initiative is part of the male role, and that he must be brazen about it if necessary, because the female would always be somewhat restrained. Although he had experienced some dramatic female initiative as a youth, it had occurred prior to complete psychosexual development and the full maturation of his analytical abilities, and thus lacked existential credibility.

N's magnetic attractiveness to men and the manner in which she threw herself into an apparently monogamous affair (on her part) with Lorenzostein (although Perk's records and comments indicate that Lorenzostein later had grave concerns about N's fidelity, but this may only have been a symptom of his developing paranoia and his impending mental decline), despite the fact that N knew that Lorenzostein was married to R and that they had three children at the time, revealed to Lorenzostein, for the first time in such a clear manner, that it is the female who does the choosing and that the male, if he turns out to have normal capabilities, merely responds appropriately to those subtle female entreaties which are made below the level of consciousness.

Yet, he knew, or in the process of acquiring normal human maleness had come to know, that he, as a male, had to market himself appropriately to females. Not being blessed with classical beauty, and being unable to display his most engaging physical attribute in everyday social intercourse due to the constraints of the times, Lorenzostein had learned, or thought he had learned, that the socially-appropriate desirable females want someone whose life's work was interesting, who had an engaging personality, and who was empathetic. Ultimately, the very best females also needed a male who could give them sexual pleasure, preferably through the medium of a large and active penis which came attached to a reasonably attractive body equipped with lips and a tongue that had some sense of the requirements of the female mouth, breasts, and thighs (and their other anatomical treasures) as well as hands that were also generous in their treatment of the female torso and its various nooks and crannies.

So Lorenzostein, having concluded that women were the ultimate coin of the realm, the ultimate form of wealth, had gone about making himself into a person who would be successful in acquiring these riches. Because a man's material wealth was of little importance to him and did not seem important to females during their younger wilder years, our hero tended to dismiss pecuniary strength as an aspect of his marketability. It was only after several blistering affairs with married women when he was in his mid-20s that Lorenzostein came to realize that considerations of financial stability and social position were usually of paramount concern to females in making marital decisions, although it did not influence their choice of lovers nor the men they chose to father their children.

From Perk's notes we can see that N was an extremely demanding mistress (as all good mistresses are), insisting that she have, at least during the summer academic break, two full days of the young academic's time, irrespective of his scholarly needs and obligations. It is also abundantly clear, and here Perk seemed to become excessive, even obsessional, in his descriptions, that N was extremely demanding in bed and had a near hysterical need for almost continuous copulation -- which Lorenzostein made every effort to quench. Yet, it seems that in N, Lorenzostein had found his match and Perk's files on both our hero and on N are replete with Lorenzostein's lamentations about N's emotional intensity and lability, and her need for physical and sexual intimacy in virtually all settings irrespective of the social consequences for Assistant Professor Lorenzostein.

It appears that N, given the emotional and sexual frenzy of her hysterical female condition, wanted, no needed, Lorenzostein to come into her immediately upon entering her apartment (invariably in the upright position), and that she was usually dressed in such subtly provocative ways when our hungry hero arrived (flaunting her full breasts in ill-fitting flannel shirts, or with skirts that graphically accentuated the vision of ecstasy that lay in the immediate future), that he had no power to do anything except comply - which he did as forcefully as possible, given that particular orientation and the natural forces of gravity.

Perk's notes and comments then become very copious for it seems that following their initial act *a pied,* they immediately relocated to N's bed where she demanded, and was provided with, the full fury of Lorenzostein's multi-dimensional offense by presenting her considerable wares in the most tantalizing manners that are imaginable to the mind of man or, for that matter, adolescent boy.

What N required of him, and what Lorenzostein delivered, were apparently incredible acts of romantic carnage. Perk's notes, which could not possibly be precise in this matter, are highlighted by constant reference to "copious amounts of thick, rich semen," endless orgasms, pleads of not to stop, references to "front door-rear door," and gagging and washing it down with inexpensive New York State champagne. There is no direct reference to the size of our hero's penis in these notes, but it seems to be an implicit assumption that his gargantuan stick was an extremely important dimension of N's relationship with him, and that it accounted for a significant part of her continuing attraction to, and satisfaction, with him -- although Lorenzostein did have other endearing characteristics.

In his notes, apparently taken directly from Lorenzostein's descriptions of the details of his sexual relationship with N, Perk frequently employs the term "cock" and "tits" in lieu of penis and breasts and often embellishes these nouns with highly descriptive adjectives which seem more likely to be of his choosing than those that were probably provided by our more placid friend. Again, these excesses appear to reflect Perk's growing obsession with N and with Lorenzostein's apparent ability to have his way with a host of highly desirable women, and is an additional indication of Perk's growing instability.

CHAPTER 6 THE DEPARTMENT OF SHITOLOGY AT U-TRASH

Lorenzostein came to U-TRASH in the mid-1970s as Assistant Professor in the Department of Shitology. He had recently received his doctorate degree from the University of Pleasant, a prestigious research university in Pleasantown in the east mid-central part of the country, and had been married to R for about five years. Their third child was born during their initial year in Trashtown. Lorenzostein's fateful relationship with N was to begin during the second half of his first year at U-TRASH. He was in his mid-30s at this time and full of professional enthusiasm and joie de vivre. As a graduate student at U-P he had had many excellent affairs (with fellow graduate students and some undergraduates, but mostly with young married women and also with older married women up to their 50s), and he had every expectation that in liberal Trashtown his life would continue along the same semi-idyllic trajectory. It was only after many years at U-TRASH, and as a resident of Greater Metropolitan Trashtown, that our friend learned the difference between political liberality and social liberality. He also learned the difference between being a graduate student in a prestigious private research university and an employee in a third-rate state university that is located in a part of a state that has a large politically-dominant religious group and which has a politically-appointed administrative bureaucracy primarily composed of members of that politically-dominant religious group.

Lorenzostein was pleased to receive an offer of a position at U-TRASH, despite the fact that it was not a leading research institution. Trashtown was a major academic center with many universities, a rich cultural life, and a liberal political tradition, and was frequently referred to as the Pathens of Pamerica. U-TRASH seemed like a reasonable place to work and Trashtown seemed to be a good place to raise a family.

He was originally attracted to shitology as an academic discipline because it encompasses the holistic study of persons, and the Department of Shitology at U-TRASH had a small-sized faculty of 16 members who appeared to have good academic qualifications. It wasn't Parvard, or Big State University at Bay, or the University of the Bulls, or Orchard and Arbor University, but it seemed, at least geographically, to be a reasonable place to raise a family with R and to begin his career in shitology. From his undergraduate years in Trashtown, Lorenzostein remembered the female population as being open and avant-garde, and he anticipated an unbroken continuation of the female companionship that he had experienced as a graduate student in Pleasantown. Unfortunately, Lorenzostein would come to experience the uncomfortable effect of the rise of political correctness on his social life, and come to see the distinction between the female population and social environment in an elite private university in a city with a tolerant religious tradition in the early to mid-1970s, and the female population and social environment in a third-rate state university in the late-1970s, and thereafter, in a city with a puritanical cultural tradition and an intolerant dominant religious group. He would also come to see the destruction of collegiate life as he had come to know it in his early years as a graduate student and academician, as the tradition of academically qualified professors serving limited terms as high-level administrators was replaced by a management tradition in which politically-connected careerist administrators, frequently with limited academic qualifications, created long-enduring academic bureaucracies of politically-connected lower level career administrators, with the careerist needs of this bureaucracy ultimately replacing the best interests of the institution.

Lorenzostein's early years in the Department of Shitology at U-TRASH were relatively harmonious. The Trashtown campus had only been created in the mid-1960s and most of the faculty in shitology were newly minted Ph.D.s who had been hired in the early to mid-1970s. He began to sense tensions in the Department in the early 1980s, around the time that he was successfully promoted to Associate Professor, with tenure, and more intensely shortly thereafter when the University adopted a policy whereby 50 per cent or more of a faculty member's annual salary increase was allocated on the basis of "merit," with each department individually deciding how merit would be determined. This greatly increased tensions among the generally underpaid members of the Department of Shitology as faculty members became pitted against one another in the process of defining what was 'meritorious' and in attempting to create an equitable system, or undermine the creation of such a system, for distributing these merit increases. This, and a later administration-initiated imposition of a more managerial form of governance in place of a collegial form of governance, led to vicious, but subtle infighting in the Department and the creation of a class of politically-connected 'winners' and another class of politically weak 'losers' within the Department.

Political labeling, intrigue, and politically-based character assassination increased markedly in the Department beginning in the late 1980s and extending into the 1990s as the cohort of faculty who had been promoted to the rank of Associate Professor of in the late 1970s and early 1980s began to position themselves, and undermine their possible competitors (with the aid of their faculty and administrative mentors and supporters), for promotion to Professor, the highest academic rank.

Political connections, not academic standing, was the most important factor in the competition among the Associate Professors for promotion to the exalted rank of Professor, and entrance into this select group was jealously guarded by the existing members of that social class. There was an informal power hierarchy in the Department of Shitology, with Red Grant on top and Fey Nayward the distantly second most influential member of the Department. Both were full Professors and established scholars, although neither was a truly major person in the field of shitology. Red was the most forceful and openly aggressive personality (the 900-pound gorilla in the Department), but his concerns mainly were related to controlling the merit system and gouging as much merit monies as he possibly could for himself. As a consequence, his salary rivaled that of the mid-to-upper level administrators, the social group within the University with which he identified. Although Fey had a less openly forceful personality, his influence within the Department was more subtle and widespread as he tended to stay in the background and appear neutral while exerting his nefarious designs through his professionally-acquired skill in labeling individuals as deviant (he was an academic expert on social labeling) and in manipulating and using others within the Department to do his biddings. Any independent voice, like that of our hero, that questioned the power structure, and how it had undermined democratic principles within the Department, was mercilessly attacked, relentlessly labeled as deviant in some way within the Department and throughout the University by Fey, Red, and their associated sycophants and water carriers, and ultimately squashed.

This is the situation in which our friend Lorenzostein found himself from the mid-1970s to the late 1990s. The political intrigue within the Department of Shitology during this period of time was of great interest to the Principal Investigator in outer space, for it created a highly charged work context in which Lorenzostein's emerging psychosexual personality would have to be worked out. However, it was the development of that personality in the context of the marital relationship that was of greatest interest to the P.I. Thus, the interactions between Lorenzostein's marriage to R, his growing family, his many affairs (particularly those that had the greatest effect on his psychosexual development and were most long-lasting), his work situation and the conflicts within it, his psychotherapy with Dr. Perk, and the changing cultural context of Trashtown and in Pamerica in the last quarter of the 20th century, were the objects of greatest research interest to the Principal Investigator. Our continuing story will attempt to portray the composite picture that emerged from these scientific investigations.

For purposes of clarity for the reader it is useful that we list the most salient members of the Department of Shitology at U-TRASH and their respective academic ranks in the late 1980s and early 1990s. Professors: Red Grant and Fey Nayward; Associate Professors: Lorenzostein, JB Hawkblack, Buck Schmuckperson, Vladimir Haverford, Babs Grabit, , Moe Moneyski, Kimiko Tamika, and Shenzi Rafel; Lecturer: Kusie Nobody; Departmental Secretary/Administrative Assistant: Junk Yard D.

Shitology, being the holistic study of persons, was an inherently interesting subject to teach and Lorenzostein had a variety of research interests which were generally fulfilling. U-TRASH did not have a graduate program in shitology, so Lorenzostein did not have bright-eyed graduate students to help him carry out his research, but had to depend on less-reliable undergraduate research assistants. This was not a desirable situation, but did not create intolerable problems in his early years at U-TRASH when there were a number of excellent undergraduate students like N and Gavid Betts. However, later on, as shitology became a less attractive undergraduate major due to a decrease in the employment prospects in the field, Lorenzostein found himself in competition with JB Hawkblack, the other member of the Department of Shitology in his research subspecialty, to attract good undergraduate students. More precisely, our friend found that Hawkblack was engaged in a systematic effort to lure Lorenzostein's best students away from him, and thus weaken his research program. One way in which he accomplished this was by developing strong personal friendships with these students that had the contrived purpose of pulling them out of our hero's research orbit and into his own, or nowhere, just so that their work with Lorenzostein, and their contributions to his research efforts, would be compromised. This was part of an overall strategy, originally conceived and coordinated by Fey Nayward: to weaken Lorenzostein's research productivity; to use student acolytes to harass our poor hero in class and criticize his teaching; and to defame him and marginalize him, all with the express purpose of preventing Lorenzostein from ever being promoted to Professor.

As noted above, Lorenzostein had had begun his rather torrid relationship with N during his first year at U-TRASH. Although he tried to be somewhat discreet about this affair, N had rather strong needs to make the relationship more public as a way of elevating her own status within the Department from that of a mere student to that of a student who was engaged in a fairly serious relationship with one of the three or four desirable male faculty members in Shitology. One cannot over-estimate the importance of this identification to an up-and-coming young woman during the waning years of the politically incorrect late 1970s, before the full rise of feminist totalitarianism. Lorenzostein's relationship with N also became common social knowledge as a result of Hawkblack's relationship with Wari Maters, one of

N's friends and a fellow student in the Department of Shitology. Thus, through Hawkblack, the entire department knew of Lorenzostein's involvement with N. The Administration of U-TRASH also learned of this relationship as a consequence of the ministrations of JB, Fey, and other runts and small-penised doody wee wees in the Department of Shitology and elsewhere.

We should also probably say something about N's possible relationship with other members of the faculty in the Department of Shitology, as Lorenzostein became preoccupied with this prospect during the fourth year of their relationship, when N was approaching graduation and about a year before they broke off seeing one another on a regular basis. Vladimir was actually the first member of the Department to have N in his class, and it was apparent to Lorenzostein from his actions that he was making a play for her. This was later confirmed by N, who maintained that Vladimir seemed to be going through the motions of seeing her and of showing up at her apartment, but, according to her, he never really pursued anything beyond the preliminaries and N, at a later date, insisted that they had never had a relationship.

JB Hawkblack was a different story, and Lorenzostein became increasingly aware of the likelihood that he was involved with N. Peck's notes are copious on this issue and disparage Lorenzostein for his paranoid fears and suspicions. Whereas Vladimir never purposefully inflamed our friend's concerns about the possibility that he was involved with N, JB took sadistic pleasure (it turned out that he was a closeted bisexual and a pedophile) in raising questions in our hero's mind that he, Hawkblack, might be seeing N, and took almost greater pleasure in gathering as much detail as he could about Lorenzostein's relationship with N – from his girlfriend Wari Maters and through a systematic program of tapping Lorenzostein's telephones, filming and recording his assignations with women, and relentlessly stalking the so-called deviant at all times.

JB was a grown man with a level of emotional maturity of a sixteen year old, who had never been married, and who was clearly repulsed by children and the care that they obviously required. He had been in the Pamerican military in Southeast Pasia and had been involved in various aspects of intelligence, counter-espionage, and electronic surveillance. JB viewed himself as a swashbuckling secret agent 0-0-HAWKBLACK, in the mold of Thames Bland, and had a go-go, action-addicted adolescent personality that was subordinate to and sought direction from established authority, like a lieutenant from a captain. Another of JB's engaging characteristics was his compulsive need to have a clearly labeled enemy against whom he could direct his psychopathic sexually-based hostility in a socially appropriate way.

As a secret pedophile and closeted bisexual, whose primary sexual attraction was to young boys of approximately 10 to 14 years of age, JB had a near hysterical need to create the impression that he was the biggest ladies' man on the U-TRASH campus, and most certainly within the Department of Shitology. This apparent womanizing served to deflect social suspicion away from his more satisfying social proclivities involving young boys. He felt particularly threatened by our bearded hero because our gentle friend obviously had, in N, the most visually desirable woman in the University, and possibly in the entire world known to civilized persons. Hawkblack was apparently threatened by the fact that Lorenzostein had the emotional depth and social personality to be able to maintain a marriage with a wife and family and to simultaneously carry on an affair with such a splendid full-titted Viking Goddess as N. This somehow undermined, in the warped cavities of his psychopathic personality, JB's own sense of self worth and engendered in him an uncontrollable sadistic need to marginalize Lorenzostein and destroy him totally, both psychologically and physically.

The tall, bearded, wild eyed, slightly socially awkward Lorenzostein, who had the appearance of a 1960s radical or Pranian revolutionary and a rather innocent and straightforward manner (although a bit unconventional by the standards of Trashtown in the 1980s and 1990s), was a convenient object of politically correct scorn who could easily be isolated and demonized by his enemies within the Department of Shitology. Furthermore, Lorenzostein was soon marginalized within the eyes of the University Administration (which over the years had become more blatantly controlled by the dominant religious group) due to the concerted actions of JB Hawkblack, Fey Nayward, Red Grant, Buck Schmuckperson, Vladimir Haverford, Babs Grabit, Moe Moneyski, Kusie Nobody, and a parade of assorted titless and dickless wonders that inhabited the halls of U-TRASH.

Our somewhat naïve friend frequently wondered why he was the object of such concerted scorn from within the Department of Shitology and he carefully tried to assess his own role in this process. What was he doing wrong that elicited such hostility? What problem did he have in "getting along" that led to this hostility and social isolation? This apparent lack of fit into his work setting, and his growing conflicts and doubts about his marriage to R, began to create profound uncertainties that were sometimes exaggerated into paranoid fears. The proximate event that led Lorenzostein to seek therapy with Dr. Perk was when R found out about his relationship with N. This was the first time that R had allowed herself to consciously recognize that her husband was involved with other women and it precipitated a period of extreme emotional turmoil in their marriage, which at that time harbored four children. Although his relationships with R and N were the main foci of his therapy with Perk, Lorenzostein also began (at least in his own mind and later with his conversations with K, his Pinglish mistress) to attempt to evaluate the psychological factors involved not only in his relationships with R and N, but also the psychodynamics of his workplace setting in the Department of Shitology.

Lorenzostein was an effective and popular teacher in the Department of Shitology, and no one could fault him for that. He was a recognized scholar in his little corner of shitology. He had published a fair amount and his work was well-received. He edited a respectable journal. He served on departmental and university committees and proposed a significant number of initiatives, most of which were roundly criticized by the Shitology faculty or ignored by the Administration. It was after two of his curricula initiatives, both of which he felt were quite thoughtful, were harshly criticized in a Shitology faculty meeting in the early 1990s that Lorenzo began to realize that the problem was not him, but that it lay within the cultural milieu of the Department of Shitology at U-TRASH and the unusual array of character disorders that were, largely by chance, represented in the Shitology faculty.

The rise, during the 1980s, of authoritarian political correctness and totalitarian feminism and the near total disappearance of democratic traditions in the University, coupled with a more muscular expression of its hegemony by the dominant religious group at U-TRASH (and in Trashtown), all contributed to the growth of a sanctimoniously intolerant social environment in which certain socially defined deviants (Lorenzostein, for his whole being; Kimiko Tamika, for her supposedly poor teaching but really because she had high academic standards, was a foreigner, and was deferential and easily intimidated; Shenzi Rafel, for his supposedly poor teaching and for vague allegations of sexual predation) were accused (as in pitchcraft) and judged to be defective (or deviant) solely on the basis of allegations concocted by a small group of individuals. These allegations were not supported by anything that could be considered to be evidence, and the accused pitches were never given the benefit of an actual comparison, based on data such as teaching evaluations, to their colleagues in the Department of Shitology. Allegations of sexual predation on students against Lorenzostein and Shenzi were not based on actual complaints, but emanated from the Shitology faculty -- a veritable cornucopia of the greatest character disorders know to personkind.

Our rather relaxed and easy going friend began to realize that he did not "fit in" because the shitologists would not allow him to fit in. He was one of the chosen "losers" who would provide slave labor teaching in the Department of Shitology, and who would never receive any substantial recognition for his accomplishments in terms of merit increases (thus his salary was unusually low despite his high standing in the field of shitology), or in terms of stature in the Department or the University. This was quite perplexing to Lorenzostein since, as an Earth Dominant Social Form Probe to the Pnited Ptates, he had assimilated the democratic traditions of that country and had applied them in a literal manner as a guide to his everyday life. The apparently complete failure of these principles in his workplace environment in the Department of Shitology at U-TRASH caused him great anxiety, as did his difficulties in his marriage to R. His marital problems had a more obvious cause, although Lorenzostein was not completely aware of it, in that our frazzled friend was equipped with an unusually large and autonomous penis due to the additive or multiplicative effects of a number of minor programming errors by the Principal Investigator in outer space. Lorenzostein sought to apply his analytical mind, trained in highly textured thick shitological analyses, to these complex social issues. This led to a number of insights that were primarily achieved by placing his tongue or his nose, more precisely the ventral portion of his nose with the nostrils in the completely flared position, on the distal portion of the clitoris of an attractive and socially appropriate female and then: 1) flexing and extending his head rapidly in a cephalo-caudal direction; 2) rotating his head rapidly in a counter-clockwise direction; and 3) gently, or forcefully, driving the tip of his tongue and/or nose in a direction determined by the degree of satisfaction garnered from the ensuing auditory clues. These insights will be discussed more fully below.

CHAPTER 7 COMING OF AGE IN THE DEPARTMENT OF SHITOLOGY

By applying his highly analytical mind to the disparate threads of the situation, Lorenzostein had come to what he felt was a fair understanding of the sociocultural dynamics in the Department of Shitology at U-TRASH. Careful, impartial social analyses was how he made order out of the inexplicable chaos of everyday life, for he was a scientist and could not turn to reassuring religious explanations as guides for social action. Within this highly textured context our hero, through brute intellectual force, generated a non-paranoid conceptual paradigm that he felt gave meaning to the social flow in the Department of Shitology. The primary conceptual theme within this flow analysis was his insight that when deviant minds find themselves together in a social group, the potential for the development of a highly deviant and dysfunctional small group culture (*D*) is a function of the deviant constant (d = .696969) raised to the p th power, in which p is the proportion of individuals who are deviants. Thus in a small social group with 11 principal members, like the Department of Shitology, of whom seven are completely deviant doody wee wees, $D = .696969^{.6363} = .7947$, which is an extremely high probability that the social group will be deviant and dysfunctional. Lorenzostein's second insight involved the effect of the Administrative culture of the University on the culture at the level of the department. He was able to show that the above probability that a small group departmental culture would become deviant and dysfunctional would double if either the President, Dean, or Sub-Sub Dean was a deviant, and would triple if two of the above individuals were certifiable deviants. Based on this thick analysis, and his unique ability to assign valid deviancy estimates to all members of the Department of Shitology and the Administration, our ingenious friend was able to proceed with the empirical analyses described below.

Lorenzo's Main Enemies

JB Hawkblack

We have seen that Hawkblack was an Associate Professor who craved to be promoted to full Professor and who sought to prevent our humble and gentle hero, Lorenzostein, from being promoted to this highly desired, sought after, and exalted position. Within the context of his peligion, JB had been named after Paint JB, from the Pew Pestament portion of the Pible. And it was Paint JB who had slain Patan and who weighed the worthiness of souls to enter the heavenly abode in this popular fairy tale. Unfortunately, for the world, and for sweet Lorenzostein in particular, our present-day JB had developed a delusional identification with his namesake and viewed himself as the righteous dispenser of divine justice not only against Lorenzostein, but also against members of various low technological level nationalist indigenous groups in his role as O-O-HAWKBLACK in the military-industrial complex. We also have seen that JB was nasty to our dear friend because he, JB Hawkblack, was a deviant. Lorenzostein was not threatened by JB and his various accomplishments. He did not care if Hawkblack had bedded down three thousand of the loveliest maidens, possibly even Visigoth princesses, within the last month, or week, or day. More power to him! Whether he did or didn't, Lorenzostein never thought about it. It did not threaten him because, although he had not copulated with three thousand princesses in the recent past, he did have a highly charged sexual and emotional relationship with a woman, N, which was meaningful to him (despite her emotional liability and at times near-hysteria), and he also had a meaningful sexual and emotional relationship with R, his wife. So, he did not covet anything that JB had, whether they were Visigoth princesses or young boys. Nor was Lorenzostein judgmental about JB's sexual preferences, or the sexual preferences of anyone else, male or female. That was their business, and nobody else's business! However, our gentle hero certainly did not condone pedophilia and was troubled by the rumors he heard from students and others that Hawkblack and his gaggle of bisexual military counter-insurgency friends were routinely involved with young boys and had abducted young girls and kept them as sex slaves.

Lorenzostein certainly did resent JB's attempts to label him, Lorenzostein, as a sexual predator for having an affair with a 23-year-old student, while he, JB Hawkblack, and many other faculty members including six in the Department of Shitology and many administrators, had engaged in varied and florid sexual relationships with students or colleagues. He was thus labeled as a sexual predator solely because he, Lorenzostein, was: not a member of a gang; not a bisexual pedophile like some of them; not a member of the dominant religious group like most of them; not a back-slapping crook and cheat like all of them; not an ultra-leftist, politically correct, pro-totalitarian feminist castrate like the large minority of them; and not a sucker up to those in authority merely because they have the keys to the cookie jar like all of them. And because, despite all of the above, he had the audacity to have a torrid affair with a big titted, amply caboosed Viking Goddess (that was known to all thanks to O-O-HAWKBLACK) although he gave the appearance of being happily married.

JB's militaristic sadism was also conflated with his sexual ambivalence and the obvious adolescent age beyond which his personality had failed to develop. In addition to spreading gossip about Lorenzostein's relationship with N, and doing what he could to disparage our friend's teaching and interfere with his ability to involve students in his research program. JB's favorite pastimes were: 1) to engage in surveillance of Lorenzostein by tapping his work and home telephones and by having his weird military and personal 'friends' follow and stalk Lorenzostein; and 2) to try to entrap Lorenzostein at U-TRASH and elsewhere in compromising situations with women in the period of time after our hero's relationship with N had ended. Lorenzostein was incredulous that Hawkblack and his obviously deviant 'friends' would put so much time and effort into these childish attempts to keep him under surveillance and entrap him with a woman. What were these hysterical adolescent sadomasochistic militaristic shitcakes trying to accomplish? Did they think that he would attempt to ravish some tasty student provocateur in his office?

Although out-of-marriage sexual relations may have been technically in violation of some very ancient law, Lorenzostein was quite certain that this law was routinely violated by a large minority of the population in cosmopolitan as well as rural settings. And he even did not care if Hawkblack and his small-penised doody wee wee friends violated an equally ancient law by placing their miniscule penises into one another's cavities, nooks, and crannies. As far as Lorenzostein was concerned, JB Hawkblack could do whatever his little black heart desired with whomever his little black heart desired to do it with -- male or female, animal, vegetable, or mineral! It was obviously not an issue of Lorenzostein doing anything that was much different than that done by other people. But, it was an issue of our gentle hero having the misfortune of being in the same academic department with JB Hawkblack, and having the winged deviant become threatened by his, Lorenzostein's, perfection. This led to our friend becoming the object of JB's sadistic psychopathological fixation. The only difference between Lorenzostein and Hawkblack, or anyone else for that matter, was that Lorenzostein, although he did not flaunt his sexuality, did not conceal it. In contrast, the true sexual perverts like JB, Fey and others at U-TRASH, lived very florid sexual lives, but they lived them in secret, and they viciously attacked ingenuous Lorenzostein as a way of creating a veneer of moral sanctimony in order to deflect social suspicion away from themselves. While our sweet friend didn't care what JB Hawkblack did or did not do, Hawkblack was a relentless stalker of Lorenzostein in an attempt to find the smallest morsel of incriminating, or even humorously personal, information about our gentle friend.

Fey Nayward

After JB, Fey Nayward was the other principal small-penised doody wee wee nemesis of Lorenzostein. He was a complete contrast to Hawkblack, although they both were closeted bisexuals and pedophiles and shared a near-hysterical contempt for Lorenzostein. JB was an obvious frenetic adolescent personality with a compulsive addiction to preposterous surveillance intrigues that had the goal of entrapping Lorenzostein in a compromising situation with a woman that would be the proximate cause of his social disgrace and his removal from the University. Fey had the same goals, but was an established scholar and presented himself as a person of exceptional uprightness, behavioral restraint, and soft-spoken academic culturedness. No one would ever suspect that Fey Nayward was the biggest split personality, pitchcraft- practicing deviant in the Department of Shitology.

Perk, when he was first somewhat sympathetic to Lorenzostein and his plight, referred to Fey Nayward as "The Fagster" in recognition of what he saw as Fey's main character disorder and the consequent behavior that it produced. This was, in Perk's terms, his near mythical ability to do harm in the most subtle and conniving ways as a consequence of his hysterical need to conceal something about himself and to project his hidden perversions onto another member of the social group by labeling him as deviant. Perk pointed out that Nayward had a need to take a subtly primary role in condemning the accused individual and assuring his (it had to be a male, as male gender identification was what was conflicting to Fey) punishment. Perk, bristling with the erudition of his training in transcultural psychiatry, referred to Fey as "The Fagster," which referred to his conceptualization of the generic personality type. He maintained that "The Fagster" is a postmodern personality construct found in industrialized societies in which science has replaced religion as the main social organizing principle, and is analogous to the personality structure of individuals who accused others of pitchcraft in societies where magic and religion were the principle foci around which social life was constructed.

JB and Fey were similar in the basic way that they were threatened by Lorenzostein's exuberant heterosexuality, as they were both lacking something in that area. However, they had dealt with it quite differently. JB had cultivated the macho image of 0-0-HAWKBLACK, his delusional version of Thames Bland, the clean-cut, good-guy action hero who would root out Lorenzostein's bearded, wild-eyed, Viking Goddess despoiling sexual deviancy. Fey, in contrast, was no less fixated on destroying our hero and eradicating the sense of uncontrolled female arousal that followed our amiable friend's every step. However, Nayward's style was much more subtle than crass entrapment attempts. Fey's way was more complete, comprehensive, and total. It involved influencing and manipulating the entire Shitology faculty to turn against Lorenzostein. To oppose and criticize our gentle friend at every little step, with respect to every little initiative, committee report, honors student, merit determination, grant application, or whatever. Anything that Lorenzostein did was to be directly belittled or criticized, or minimized, by as large a segment of the social group as was possible to recruit into this endeavor, and this criticism was to take place primarily within the monthly faculty meeting of the Department of Shitology. Within that face-to-face context, any request or idea that Lorenzostein put forward was to be rejected and viciously belittled or criticized by the core group of deviants that Fey had woven together. And they would relentlessly disparage and demonize Lorenzostein to the U-TRASH administrators who knew little more about our quiet, hard-working friend than what they heard from the politicos in the Shitology faculty.

As was revealed above, both Nayward and Hawkblack were closeted bisexuals. This had been confirmed by Perk's own investigation and analysis. Furthermore, it was quickly clear to Perk that both Fey and JB were primarily pedophiles who had a strong preference for short, slight attractive blond boys between about 10 and 14 years of age. They had actually been somewhat open about their pedophilic sexual preferences back in the 1970s, when this was socially fashionable and rarely an object of legal inquiry. Perk concluded that they were both driven into the closet by the appearance of the scarlet mark of AIDS in the early 1980s, the growing condemnation of pomosexuality by the religious right, and the development of aggressive political correctness in the 1980s and 1990s which took a strong position against child exploitation. Furthermore, there were persistent rumors that

Hawkblack and his fellow patriots and guardians of democracy and freedom in his special counter-insurgency unit were involved in kidnapping, sexual enslavement, and trafficking of young girls. Perk agreed with our friend, or led our hero to the insight, that by demonizing Lorenzostein and labeling him as a deviant both Fey and JB sought desperately to gain social recognition as 'normal' for themselves by assuming a public posture at U-TRASH of sanctimonious moral purity to deflect any possible questions, or social murmur, about their own proclivities. What Perk continually emphasized to Lorenzostein in these early years when he was sympathetic to his cause, was that Nayward's and Hawkblack's underlying anxieties about being exposed were so great that it was psychically necessary for them to continually and relentlessly demonize Lorenzostein as a sexual predator and distinguish themselves from him by being his most prominent accusers and harshest judges. Perk pointed out to Lorenzostein that, in contrast to Fey and JB and their coterie of followers in the Department of Shitology, other faculty members at U-TRASH who were psychologically normal themselves did not take hostile, or any, positions in denouncing Lorenzostein for his relationship with N.

Perk also helped our friend understand how his functional psychological analysis applied to the Administration's attitude toward Lorenzostein as well as that of the shitologists. In Perk's view, Lorenzostein was only condemned by President Herpie Smerpy, Dean Mess Luogano, and Sub-Sub Dean Henry Halfdickless because the Administration needed a scapegoat, or scapegoats, such as Shenzi

Rafel and Kimiko Tamika, two other ethnic-religious minorities who had been similarly condemned. The reason that the Administration needed scapegoats was to demonstrate to the Legislature and their Board of Trustees that they were actually doing something as high-level academic administrators (rooting out the sexual deviants and the poor teachers from among the faculty), for they had very little else to demonstrate in terms of accomplishments at the University.

By incredible coincidence, Perk had participated in a clinical symposium on ethical issues at a national conference in psychiatry with a group of prominent academic psychiatrists that touched on exactly these circumstances that existed at U-TRASH. At this meeting one of the participants discussed two of his patients, who he described as high level administrators at a nearby state university, whom Perk recognized from his many conversations with Lorenzostein as being President Herpie Smerpy and Dean Mess Luogano from U-TRASH. According to this distinguished psychiatrist, Herpie had worked her way into, and up, the administrative hierarchies of several universities, culminating with her appointment at President of U-TRASH, by engaging in serial sexual relations with male administrators and legislators who were in superior positions of power in relation to her and who could advance her career.

Herpie also had a sexual relationship with Mess Luogano, whom she appointed as Dean. In turn, Mess and his Sub-Sub Dean Henry Halfdickless had both been carrying on affairs with Shelley Flash, a junior member of the Humanities faculty whom they had promoted quickly from Assistant to Associate Professor and had then created a new, well-paying administrative position for her as Director of International Exchanges.

It was clear to Perk that many members of the Administration at U-TRASH, as well as many members of the Department of Shitology, had been involved in some form of non-traditional sexual relationship at one time or another. In Perk's view at this time, our hero's relationship with N differed from these other academic relationships only in the degree to which his relationship to N, and personal life in general, were subjected to such intense scrutiny and surveillance by 0-0-HAWKBLACK, the University Political Correctness Police, and the Administration-enlisted State Police Sexual Predators Unit. Consequently, every little detail of Lorenzostein's personal life, which was probably not all that different from the personal lives of other faculty or administrators at U-TRASH, became known.

Kusie Nobody

Kusie Nobody was a woman of about 67 years of age who was a Lecturer and the only person in the Department who did not have a doctorate degree. She had been granted a part-time, non-professorial position within the Shitology faculty during the early days in the 1960s when the Trashtown campus of U-TRASH was first formed. This was due to the influence of her husband, Clarence, who was a prominent member of a natural science department and a politically well-connected individual. Kusie had no doctoral degree, limited or no publications, and no national or international recognition in any little corner of shitology. Nevertheless, she had been in the

Department for nearly 30-years and despite the fact that she had very low academic rank or recognition, she had assumed an air of authority and expertise in shitology and had thrown herself into the politics of the University and the Department. Consequently, most people in the University who did not know that she had the academic rank and the academic recognition of a nobody, assumed that she was a person of some stature. This was reinforced by her pushy personality, good social networking skills, and her ability to present herself as a warm mother figure despite the fact that she was actually a ruthless ward politician.

Kusie was the departmental gossip, finger pointer, and social manipulator. Besides not having come to terms with her lack of academic accomplishment, Kusie had never dealt with the fact that her prominent and charming husband, Clarence, had had many affairs in the University, including a long-time fairly public relationship with a female colleague in his department and many affairs with students, including a torrid long-term relationship with a Pavanese graduate student who was working under his supervision. Rather than recognize the fact that her husband of many years was screwing around right in front of her, and either doing something about it or accepting it, Kusie blocked out and denied her husband's indiscretions and projected the totality of her anger, sanctimonious indignation, and hurt onto Lorenzostein for his relationship with N, the details of which had been broadcast widely by Hawkblack with her encouragement.

Vladimir Haverford

What was most striking about Vladimir

Haverford was that he had the appearance of a complete dullard, but beneath the surface was a vicious and conniving politician. Because Vladimir connivingly gave the impression of being exquisitely empathetic, Lorenzostein, at first, viewed him as a normal person despite the fact that his speech was excruciatingly slow and his thought process was ponderous and muddled in the extreme. Kusie, for example, was an hysteric whose thought process on substantive issues made little or no sense, but she got from point A to point B in a reasonable amount of time, even if the way she connected the two points lacked any logic and was obviously driven by frenzy. Haverford, on the other hand, approached an issue in such a plodding manner, that was cloaked in such an overblown sense of sincerity, that it created the impression of a carefully thought out treatise. However, his productions had no substance whatsoever because his mind had no substance whatsoever. What Vladimir did create were vague frameworks that said or did nothing and accomplished nothing. However, these nothings were created in a ponderous, lengthy, faux-sincere, faux-inclusionary, manner that was calculated to win him a modicum of approval as a good boy and a hard working departmental member in the eyes of the senior movers and shakers and politicians in shitology -- Red, Fey, and Kusie -- and thus position himself as a worthy candidate for promotion to the rank of full Professor.

Another of Vladimir's endearing characteristics was that he was a doctrinaire Parxist, or, more precisely, a Ptalinist -- the highly civilized form of leftist politics that was politically dominant at U-

TRASH. This was not a particularly intellectualized stance with a consistent politico-economic analysis. Instead, it was a vague hodge-podge of ad hoc positions based on a patronizing and sanctimonious advocacy of minority rights. This was coupled with unequivocal support for the totalitarian feminism that reigned at U-TRASH in the 1980s and 90s. Unfortunately, there were few female victims of this imagined sexual discrimination at hyperfeminist, politically correct U-TRASH during this period of time. Nevertheless, in order to find a role for himself, and get some social mileage and brownie points out of the feminist endeavor, Vladimir became a founding member of the Sexual Harassment Committee. This committee had the main purpose of turning up imaginary male sexual predators (individuals with several of the following characteristics: possessed a penis; was not pay; had normal sexual inclinations; was not a member of the protected racial/ethnic group; was not a member of the dominant religious group; was not adequately politically correct; and was not a member of their Parxist gang).

This multi-faceted shitologist had one even more salient, or defining, characteristic. Because he was the most dim-witted of the shitologists, Haverford had developed a particular kind of adaptation. In his very first year at U-TRASH, sensing his mental limitations and cognizant of what was required to be promoted to the rank of Associate Professor with tenure, Vladimir cultivated the art of being the biggest ass kisser known to exist on the face of the Earth. The first time that our hero heard Vladimir, at a Shitology faculty meeting, launch into a lengthy oration laudatory of Red Grant's bull shit trolley car scholarship, he thought that all present would break out laughing at the crassness of Vladimir's absolute sycophantry. However, our naïve friend was amazed at how the assembled intellectuals took this all in stride without a smile on their faces or a roll of their eyes, and it was at this point that Lorenzostein learned one of the cardinal 'rules of the game' in the culture of the dysfunctional Department of Shitology at U-TRASH. That rule is that there is no 'right' or 'wrong', or even discussion of what is 'right' or 'wrong'. What there is, is blind subservience to the aggressive psychopathological shitheads who have established themselves in positions of power.

Gentle Lorenzostein provided an easy target for Vladimir which the Parxist crusader used to great effect. Being a bit intellectually challenged, Vladimir's social needs in the Department were quite similar to Kusie's. That is, how to keep himself from being at the bottom of the social pyramid. (Actually, there was no need to have a social pyramid in the Department of Shitology, there could have been a flat playing field. But, to the faux-Parxists, social justice was an abstraction that is practiced in relation to someone else, preferably in a highly patronizing manner.) Vladimir, through his participation in many of the political correct police committees at U-TRASH, was an important vehicle for transporting the label of defective and deviant, which had been given to Lorenzostein, Shenzi, and Kimiko within the Department of Shitology, and maliciously spreading it throughout the University. As a former card carrying member of the Pommunist Party of the PUSA., and an individual awash in false sincerity and sanctimonious rectitude, Vladimir was a convincing critic of our large-penised friend in the faux-Parxist, politically correct ambiance at U-TRASH. In this role he used his knowledge of Lorenzostein's relationship with N, the multi-titted goddess, and the findings of Hawkblack's surveillance of Lorenzostein to rail against our empathetic, somewhat naive, large-penised hero, with a fury that was second to none and with a level of sanctimony that was exceeded only by Kusie's.

Buck Schmuckperson

Let us now praise Buck Schmuckperson, for he, among the exalted assembly of the shitologists, was the most overbearingly pedantic individual who was so totally enraptured with his sense of learning, erudition, moral perfection, ethnic purity, and mere physical presence, that one has no choice but to appropriately crown him with the appellation of THE SCHMUCK Of All SCHMUCKS. To put it in more simple, straight-forward, terms, if ever there was a schmuck, Buck Schmuckperson was it.

One of the many problems that Lorenzostein had with shitology was that he felt that shitologists were overly pompous about their knowledge and learning and that they, even as people who had committed their lives to be educators, made little effort to make their ideas understandable in some way to others (either scholars in their broader field, students, or the general public) beyond a very small 'in-group' of similarly initiated colleagues who could speak and understand their language. Schmuckperson was the most extreme example of this self-important and academically overbearing personality among the shitologists at U-TRASH, and this characteristic did not endear him to our hero. However, our friend was a generally accepting sort and he was willing to live and let live. Furthermore, he realized that he, Lorenzostein, had a problem in this area. Lorenzostein tended to be at the other extreme of the academic pomposity continuum in that he frequently found it difficult to take his own research seriously in that it seemed to be much ado about almost nothing and an enormous amount of effort for what frequently appeared to be limited results that were read by few people and understood by even fewer. Somewhere along the line, perhaps from Camus, Lorenzostein had lost whatever interest he may have had in speaking authoritatively about anything, and he had come to the sad conclusion that language is usually used to pontificate and obfuscate rather than to communicate. The degree to which Schmuckperson carried this pompous posturing and erudite strutting was somewhere between breathtaking and comical.

The greater difficulty with Buck Schmuckperson lay in the fact that in some important aspects of his behavior he was, in Lorenzostein's view, the person in the shitology faculty who was the closest to being truly psychotic. This became particularly salient when Schmuckperson became Chair of the Department of Shitology in the early 1990s. We will discuss our hero's understandings of the terms neurotic and psychotic more fully below. For our present purposes we can say that Lorenzostein was struck by Schmuckperson's apparent inability to view issues in empirical terms so as to distinguish what was clearly fact from non-fact, or opinion, or gossip, or rumor, or mere accusation. The ferocity with which the schmucked wonder promulgated his beliefs or opinions about issues as the given truth was also astounding. Lorenzostein was trained in empirical science and, as a scholar who had one foot in the natural sciences and the other in the social sciences, he also had a healthy respect for the relativity of truth and of human beliefs. Schmuckperson had no use whatsoever for empiricism, and in conflicts over personnel matters in the department he did not see any use for evidence. It was He and He alone who knew what was right and what was wrong and who was good and who was bad. He was both the accuser and the judge. If Schmuckperson would make an accusation against another faculty member, then he was right and there was no need to present evidence or any kind of empirical or comparative data to support his assertions. If a student made an accusation against a faculty member to Schmuckperson, as Chair of the Department, and Schmuckperson disliked the faculty member, the accusation would be taken at face value and considered valid by the All-Knowing Schmuck. However, the same accusation by the same person against someone Schmuckperson liked would be dismissed out of hand. Similarly with the accuser. An accusation by someone he liked, or who he was political correctly connected to, was valid, while the same accusation against the same person (unless he disliked the accused) by someone Buck did not like, or was not political correctly connected to, would be totally dismissed.

Buck Schmuckperson, the all knowing, sanctimonious, morally pure, natural leader was not tethered by the view that accusations are merely allegations, not established facts. Or, that anonymous accusations made in unsigned letters, on walls, and in bathroom stalls, are just that -- allegations by unknown individuals who cannot be held accountable for what they say and should be treated as such, and not as established fact. Or, that accusations should be supported by evidence. Or, that the accused has the right to due process where he/she can question his/her accuser(s) and present evidence to support their case -- not merely listen to the summary judgment of the All-Knowing Schmuck.

It was the degree to which Schmuckperson saw himself as the font of all truths, the accuser and the judge, the just and morally pure natural leader, that traversed the line from that of an authoritarian personality with strong politically correct beliefs, to that of a delusional personality who had concocted a grandiose vision of himself as the omnipotent leader who has descended from the heavens to rule the land. There were other aspects of Schmuckperson's psyche that suggested that he had a personality in search of some structure. He had thrown himself full-heartedly into virtually every trendy religious (five years as a Hootist monk) and progressive cultural (communes, nativism) movement of the past 30-years, only to end up resurrecting the personality of an abusive ancestor from whom he was descended.

We need not go into any detail about how this sanctimonious schmuck participated, or orchestrated, in many of the accusations of pitchcraft against our beloved hero, and even more so against Shenzi and Timiko, and how his obvious moral purity, pompous erudition, leaderly bearing and thick-headedness were used and manipulated by Fey, Kusie, Vladimir, and JB to lend credibility to their growing cacophony about Lorenzostein and the threat posed by his oversized dick and lustful personality to all of womankind and the continued existence of civilization. That sexual excess and ethical myopia were rampant in the Department of Shitology, in the faculty as a whole, in the Administration of the University, and the country as a whole, was irrelevant. In Schmuckperson's all-knowing view, the main problem was Lorenzostein and he must be hunted down, marginalized, humiliated, and destroyed totally and completely.

Red Grant

Very little good could be said about Red Grant that he had not already said. First, Red was the self-described most "meritorious" member of the Department of Shitology. Annual salary merit increases in Shitology were calculated on the basis of a quantitative system that evaluated 'scholarship', teaching, and service to the department, university, and profession. The system was highly weighted in favor of 'scholarship', and within 'scholarship' the system did not distinguish on the basis of the prestige of the journal where an article was published or the particular press that had published a book. Furthermore, this highly quantitative system gave a disproportionate number of merit points for short articles, which could even have been published in unrefereed trade magazines. Red's area of scholarly expertise in shitology was the detailed study of trolley car schedules historically and how these schedules, themselves, provide central insights into the growth of industrialization in the Western world, class and racial divisions in developing countries, the rise of feminism cross-culturally, water temperatures in the Antarctica, the spread of bubonic plague in medieval Europe, and the future direction of the stock market. Red Grant did not shit around! His scholarly articles were highly textured thick analyses of these very important, and clearly connected, social factors, which were published in a wide variety of unrefereed trolley car driver and brakeperson magazines and trolley car enthusiast mimeo sheets. Within the Shitology Department merit system (which Red's big personality had forced down the throat of the Department against our hero's objections, which earned him Red's everlasting hatred), Red Grant was the big winner, garnering large merit salary increases each year and a salary that was far higher than anyone else's in the Department.

Red was basically asexual (according to Mrs. Grant), which was acceptable to Lorenzostein as many people are basically asexual. But Red certainly did not have an ambiguous sexual identity like Fey and JB that was threatened by our hero's penal exploits, nor did he have their pomosexually-driven need to physically dominate or emasculate our large-penised hero, or Kusie's hysterical projective needs. Red's fixation was not sex, but money and secondarily power. While Lorenzostein could rightly be accused of being greedy for sex, the coin of Red Grant's realm was money, lots of money, and his greed for this commodity matched, or exceeded, Lorenzostein's lustful requirements. Power was also important to Red, but his need for power was derived mostly from his need to control the departmental merit system to assure that he would benefit disproportionately from the way it was structured and the manner in which it was implemented. Red's considerable hostility to our friend, reaching highly elevated levels of hatred in the 1990s, was mainly a consequence of Lorenzostein's sincere attempts to make the departmental merit system fairer and his efforts to stop outright dishonesty in the way the merit procedures were implemented. But, it was decreed that Red's 250-word book reviews and short unrefereed articles were to be judged as meritorious paragons of shitological scholarship -- period! Red found common cause with Fey, Kusie, Hawkblack, Vladimir and Smuckperson in living for the day that they would see Lorenzostein mashed into the ground.

Lorenzostein realized that he was the unfortunate recipient of discriminatory and disparate treatment because he did not conceal the fact that he was from a Pewish background, because he was a threat psychologically to the small-penised doody wee wees due to his incandescent sexuality, and because of the fact that he operated in a group setting in a democratic fashion. He came to see that religious intolerance, intolerance of open sexuality, and the erosion of democratic process and the rise of authoritarianism were all significant trends in the Pnited Ptates in the late 1980s into the 1990s. At one level, Lorenzostein could understand that the group hatred of him was irrational and could only be vaguely understood in terms of how it served various individual and group needs within the dysfunctional Shitology faculty and the University, which had a politically correct ideology and a power structure totally controlled by members of the dominant religious group. Yet, our friend could never reach an understanding of how the so-called cardinal sins of 'adultery', and 'fornication' had achieved such preeminence as sins in Pamerican culture, while the equally ancient and sacred categorization of 'greed' and 'hypocrisy' as cardinal sins, to be punished by eternal damnation, were not words that were used at

U-TRASH or, apparently, in Pamerican society. Surely, Red's behavior was the epitome of greed and hypocrisy reigned supreme in Shitology and throughout U-TRASH. And the administrators were, by far, the biggest greedballs -- led by President Herpie Smerpy herself, dripping greed out of every pore in her body. To our somewhat naive, large-penised Dominant Social Form Probe from outer space, these apparent inconsistencies were not comprehensible. In his mind it seemed intuitively obvious that the sins of 'adultery' and 'fornication' were far less socially corrosive and destructive than the much more common sins of 'greed' and 'hypocrisy'. Lorenzostein wondered whether this had something to do with the development of complex societies or of capitalism itself, or if it could, perhaps, be explained on the basis of trolley car schedules in the cities of Central Europe during the 1880s.

CHAPTER 8 WHO IS THIS LORENZOSTEIN AND WHY WAS HE REALLY SENT TO US FROM OUTER SPACE?

Up to this point, it has been revealed to the reader that Lorenzostein truly was not descended from the apes, but that he had come to us from outer space; that his marriage to R was quite problematic; that he had an enormous penis through which data about certain aspects of his life on Earth were transmitted back to the Principal Investigator in outer space; that women dearly desired his picturesque apparatus and its copious mud-like production, and that this caused him great difficulties with other males who lacked his much sought after endowment; and that gentle Lorenzostein endured a hostile work place environment in which he suffered many torments and constant harassment at the hands of the small-penised doody wee wees and deviants in the Department of Shitology and in the Administration at U-TRASH.

Perk had been fairly sympathetic to our frenzied friend early in his therapy and was drawn to his analytic abilities and highly empathetic nature, although from the start he felt that Lorenzostein's views were overly complex and had geared his treatment toward assisting him in seeing social reality in a simpler more straightforward manner. Perk had seen innumerable cases of tension in the marriages of young academic couples in which one partner, usually the male, was under extreme scholarly pressure. The fact that Lorenzostein and R had five children and that R was working part-time created a typical therapeutic situation. Interrelated conflicts at home and at work were fairly common under these circumstances, and Perk was usually quite successful in rectifying these situations.

However, in the course of his treatment of our hero, Perk began to become aware of certain issues which enormously raised his level of concern. At first, he took Lorenzostein's rantings about his need for sex, his many mistresses over the years, and the variegated manner in which he had sex with N, as manifestations of 'sex as hostility' on Lorenzostein's part to the many stressful features of his life and also as a way that the young professor sought to gain control over something, women, at a time when he had little actual control over anything in his home and work environments. But, Lorenzostein's preoccupation with sex seemed to have reached monumental proportions, so to speak, as he began to reveal to Perk details about the enormous size, power, and apparent autonomy, of his gargantuan penis.

Lorenzostein had been just another male patient in whom low social status in the workplace, situational difficulties, anger, and sex were all entwined, and N was just another young thing on whom these existential issues were being worked out -- with whatever she brought to the situation being an added dimension to the whole gestalt. But, Lorenzostein's repeated references to the size and apparent power of his penis, which appeared to Perk to be highly delusional, his decadent sociobiological mutterings about female choice and female reproductive strategies, and finally, and fatefully, the 8"x10" photograph of N that he showed to Perk relatively late in his therapy, had a cumulative effect on Perk's view of our protagonist. Upon seeing the picture of N, Perk immediately, and with great passion, began to view her as an innocent girlish victim of this long-haired, bearded, wild-eyed, sexual predator who, apparently, did actually have an abnormally large penis which he used in the most nefarious manner to sexually enslave innocent maidens and married women with the expressed purpose of filling their soft moist vaginas with his mud-like slime.

After carrying out some slightly voyeuristic field work to assure himself that Lorenzostein's reported relationship with N was not a fabrication of the bearded-one's twisted mind, Perk concluded, as is clearly shown in his files and in his periodic reports to Lorenzostein's health insurance carrier, that Lorenzostein was a psychotic sexual predator of the worst kind. Perk now had continual visions of the obviously large-titted Viking Goddess and was having trouble sleeping at night. Interestingly, he began to notice that he had an almost constant erection, although tiny, and that it was quite leaky. In order to protect the innocent N from the bearded deviant, Perk pledged to himself that he would do everything within his power to assure that this large-penised madman was constrained by the full force and authority of society. Soon after submitting one of his unsympathetic insurance reports on Lorenzostein's therapy, Perk was contacted by President Herpie's office. He was offered the opportunity, which he gladly accepted, to work with the authorities to remove Lorenzostein from the University as a threat to society. In this capacity he would work with the Administration of U-TRASH, the office of Oriole Outlaw (the principal representative of the dominant religious group in Trashtown), the State Police Sexual Predator Unit, and several distinguished members of the Department of Shitology at U-TRASH (Professors Red Grant and Fey Nayward; Associate Professors JB Haverford, Vladimir Haverford, Buck Schmuckperson, Babs Grabit, and Moe Moneyski; and Lecturer Kusie Nobody). Perk's role in this endeavor was to gather, in the therapeutic setting, as much information as was possible about Lorenzostein's deviant behavior and to pass these findings on to the Administration at U-TRASH through Fey Nayward, who was the overall conceptualizer and coordinator of this democratic endeavor. Parallel efforts would be carried out by the State Police Sexual Predator Unit and by Hawkblack and his 'friends', so that Lorenzostein would be followed, observed, and kept under electronic surveillance virtually 24-hours a day. In this role, Perk would also provide a professional forensic psychiatric review of the accumulated information which would, in no uncertain terms, clearly label Lorenzostein as a total psychotic deviant sexual predator who must be removed from his position at U-TRASH, and from society altogether, for the protection of the social whole. By engaging in these modest, and low-cost, interventions, society would be insulated from the abuses and ravages of this bearded, wild-eyed sexual deviant. To this end, Perk began to collect more detailed, and less sympathetic, information about our large-penised, mud-like semen producing, hero.

The plan developed by Fey was for Perk to collect more detailed accounts from Lorenzostein on virtually all aspects of his life and for the good doctor to find the worst possible flaws in our friend's character and behavior and include these observations and analyses in his insurance reports on Lorenzostein. In this way, Lorenzostein's deviancy would be clearly labeled as such, and would be given added credibility by the unquestioned authority of the well-known Dr. Perk, an eminent psychiatrist known for his own sobriety and lack of passion. With this evidence in the records, the Administration, acting through the agencies of JB Hawkblack and the State Police Sexual Predator Unit, would endeavour to catch (more precisely, entrap) our guileless friend in one or two acts of unquestionable deviancy by having a tasty female 'student' make a rather clear, but subtle, approach to him in his office. If Lorenzostein would respond in any way whatsoever: by mounting her in his office then and there; by asking her out to lunch and then satisfying his lust off campus; or by saying anything that they, the impartial moral authorities, deemed to be suggestive, weird, or bizarre; that would constitute unquestionable grounds for removing Lorenzostein from the University. These actions would protect the Administration from lawsuits from female students who might, as a consequence of their hyper-aroused near-hysterical state, believe that they had been subjected to predatory behavior by the bearded, wild-eyed deviant. Hawkblack realized that they might not be able to get Lorenzostein to actually mount their tasty tart in his office, but, given Perk's authoritative reports and diagnosis, any strange behavior on Lorenzostein's part toward their tart should be considered a preliminary approach by him that would undoubtedly lead to consummation at some point in the very near future if not for their timely intervention.

Fey was particularly proud of his design, for it had the subtle dignity of his passive aggressive personality. He was here able to combine his academic interests in the way labeling functions as a central component of the practice of pitchcraft with his and Vladimir's commitment to 'action shitology" and its Ptalinist political goals. The urbane, professorial, buffy-haired, gentlemanly, pay in that refined manner so common in academia, Fey Nayward luxuriated in the sense of power that he derived from his ability, as the leader of this small group of 'credible' people who were insistent and incessant in their accusations, to convince the larger social group (the University community) of the validity of their claims without benefit of evidence and without allowing Lorenzostein the opportunity to ever know about, let alone respond to, their allegations.

Perk was pleased to be working with the scholarly and refined Nayward and the other members of the Shitology Department and the U-TRASH Administration in these efforts to contain Lorenzostein. In the deep recesses of his mind Perk realized that both Nayward and Hawkblack were complete deviants and pedophiles and that many of the 'big deals' in the U-TRASH Administration and the other chief players in the Shitology Department had severe character disorders at the minimum. But, they were charming and pleasant, unlike the bearded and wild-eyed Lorenzostein, and they included him as part of their somewhat exclusive social group and compensated him quite generously.

It was at this point, when Perk had become obsessed with N and our hero's relationship with her, to the detriment of his sympathies for Lorenzostein, that Perk began to see our friend's contorted personal life in a much more critical fashion. Lorenzostein's unhappiness with his sexual relationship with R was increasingly offensive and pathological to Perk. Perk had seen R and had made her an object of some of his clandestine field work, although not to the degree, or with the emotional involvement that he had investigated N. R was a beautiful, dignified woman and an obviously devoted mother and wife. She was pleasant and cheery and was respected and adored by all who knew her. What did this pervert Lorenzostein want or need? To inflict his juvenile sexual appetites on this lovely woman on a daily basis. Or in his compulsive deviant five-times-plus-a-day hostile, woman-demeaning manner? R acquiesced once a week, or every five days. What was wrong with that? Perk, himself, never had sex with Mrs. Perk and they had a perfectly compatible relationship! Lorenzostein's compulsive need for frequent, passionate (more correctly hostile and abusive) sex with his hard working wife who was burdened with much of the responsibility of raising their five young children reflected the needs of a self-absorbed sexual deviant who society must emasculate and encapsulate for the protection of all women. And perhaps more importantly, so that men may rest in peace knowing that their most valuable possessions -- their wives, women friends, mistresses, daughters, and the beautiful innocent maidens who are the wards of society -- are forever safe from the despoiling needs of this tall, bearded, wild-eyed deviant.

Perk believed that Lorenzostein's increasingly glazed-eyed rantings were not an example of male sexual hyperbole, but were a clear manifestation of his totally delusional deviant personality and his rapid psychotic decline. In the early 1990s, in the thirteenth year of our amiable hero's psychotherapy with Dr. Perk, his story began to shift, according to Perk's notes, away from complaints about his sexual relationship with R and the juvenile, exaggerated, highly idealized renditions of his relationship with the big-titted N. Beginning around this period of time, Lorenzostein's weekly sessions with Perk were dominated by his insistent claim that he was something which he called The Large-Penised Male. Apparently, Lorenzostein had come to the belief, which was only revealed in these therapeutic sessions with the honest Dr. Perk, that he, Lorenzostein, was The Large-Penised Male, which he claimed was the subject of a religious prophesy. According to Lorenzostein, as recorded in Perk's thorough notes on this subject and marginal commentary, it was prophesized somewhere in the ancient holy writings of the dominant Western religion that a leader and savior would emerge from among the mass of the people, and that this leader would come to be called The Large-Penised Male. Furthermore, according to Lorenzostein, the primary heavenly-sent mission of The Large Penis Male was to disperse voluminous amounts of fresh rich semen through the air and in the water supplies across the planet. Lorenzostein began to claim that he had come from outer space and that he had been provisioned with highly particulate weaponized spermatozoa capable of traveling great distances through hostile environments in their ceaseless quest for moist, and slightly patent, vaginas. This spermatozoa, according to our increasingly delusional hero, contained its reproductive message in the form of ZNA, and Lorenzostein maintained that it was that unique genetic material that was the source of his empathetic personality. This heavenly force propelled Lorenzostein to use his great thing to seek moist and slightly patent vaginas, and to uncontrollably spread his semen far and wide, so as to introduce, here on Earth, a new kind of people who would establish His Kingdom of Considerate Civility and Deep Personal Empathy. This, he maintained, would be a kingdom devoid of hypocrisy, where men and women, or whoever and whomever, could do as they wish, free of the hypocritical and self-righteous pursuits of the Fey Naywards, JB Hawkblacks, and Red Grants of the world.

How this idea that he was The Large-Penised Male had gotten into our friend's head is not certain, but its delusional grandiosity and perverted millennial theme were clear indications to Perk that he was now dealing with the onset of frank psychosis. Lorenzostein had confided these thoughts to his psychiatrist Dr. Perk and apparently had not spoken them to others, and Perk had not received any information from Nayward that would indicate that our hero had promulgated these ideas in public at U-TRASH or had acted in a way that reflected these delusionary beliefs. Nevertheless, after careful consultation with that paragon of moral purity Fey Nayward, Perk concluded, with total certainty, that: Lorenzostein was psychotic; that he harbored thoughts that were dangerous to society and upon which he might act; and every effort should be made to remove him from the embrace of society. More specifically: 1) he should be removed from his position at U-TRASH; 2) he should be imprisoned; and 3) he should be destroyed psychologically so that he would become such a spent man that his apparently tree-like penis would lose its sting. We should reiterate that the unbiased and honest Dr. Perk was paid very, very well for his work on this important documentary project, and that he was now invited to many high-level social events by the U-TRASH academic and administrative communities.

There was another unbearably delusional turn in Lorenzostein's behavior during this period of time, to which we alluded earlier in our story, that further consolidated Perk's belief that Lorenzostein was completely mad. Our hero still complained bitterly about his sexual relationship with R; that it was not frequent enough, or rigorous, or long-lasting, and that R seemed to be just going through the motions. However, around this time a new, and highly delusional, twist emerged. Lorenzostein originally interpreted R's alleged lack of sexual zest as being a consequence of her Praker upbringing and her rather reserved, proper, restrained personality. Now, our hero, having seen flashes of extreme, although greatly limited in time, passion in R, concluded that she was really an extremely sensual and passionate person, but that her sexual desires and preferences must lay outside of her marriage to him. Lorenzostein built up a scenario of suspicion in which he firmly believed that R was carrying on multiple sexual relations with both men and women, mainly during the middle of the workday from noon to about 3 PM when she made the transition from her morning worksite to her afternoon place of work. Furthermore, Lorenzostein firmly believed that R had multiple personalities that were totally compartmentalized from one another. Although R reassured him that she was not seeing anyone in a romantic relationship, either male or female, our increasingly muddled hero believed that the wifely, motherly, 'good', non-sexual personality to which he was married was totally compartmentalized from the risqué, adventuresome, playful, nymphomaniacal, heart-shaped earring-wearing personality that he believed R switched into when she was 'wandering', as he called it, and that the R that he knew was not capable of ever acknowledging, or even being dimly aware of, the actions of the other part or parts.

The usually unflappable Perk was appalled by Lorenzostein's cruel accusations and condemnations of his blameless wife. It was patently obvious to the font of psychiatric knowledge that the deviant Lorenzostein was clearly projecting his own desires, behaviors, and split personality onto the long-suffering R. First, she had to tolerate his juvenile philandering with his purportedly huge dick, and now she must endure the further indignity of being accused, pure-hearted as she is, of the very decadent dissipation that characterized Lorenzostein's deviant ways. This, Perk felt, was a second example of hero's moral cowardice and his totally delusional, paranoid, self-centered misogynistic behavior. Enslaving and despoiling N was bad enough, but to be such a heartless deviant that he could accuse his wronged wife of the very acts that he had inflicted on her were beyond Perk's basically upper middle class conception. Lorenzostein was clearly a morally bankrupt individual who, despite his high professional status and his apparent integration into society as a married man with a lovely wife and a family, must be destroyed immediately so that all persons -- both female and male -- may be forever insulated from his deviant ways.

CHAPTER 9 K

A third development occurred at about this same period of time which further undermined any hope that Perk may have had that Lorenzostein was a morally redeemable individual. After enduring the shitologist's tedious complaints about R and listening to his infantile tales of his enrapture and sexual exploitation of N, and to his reports of a series of brief relationships which did not seem to satisfy his sexual or emotional needs, Perk began to hear, in his weekly meetings with Lorenzostein, about a new object of his perverted affection, K, who he referred to as his Pinglish mistress. Lorenzostein's torrid relationship with K had apparently resuscitated him from the swamp of despair, and he now pursued this entanglement with the same manic enthusiasm that he had shown in his involvement with N. It was increasingly clear to the learned savant that Lorenzostein was a depressive, insecure, immature personality who could only raise himself out of the depths of his despair by fornicating incessantly with equally needy women, who Perk assumed had probably not received proper attention and love from their parents. In his particular case, our hero's depression-alleviating compulsive sexual activities and manic-paranoid frenzies had driven him to a state of paranoid, delusional, psychosis of the worst possible kind.

Park listened with near total contempt, having borne witness to his despoliation of N and indifferent dismissal of R, as the so-called Large-Penised Male ranted and raved about his new Pinglish mistress, as he so considerately called her. Tits and ass were not the issue here. Her face, although extremely attractive, and her figure, which was shapely and slender, were not her only attributes that held Lorenzostein's considerable attention. That which did warrant his particular accolades was a vagina, in the aging deviant's terms a 'flaming vagina', that, according to this manic-depressive-needy-juvenile deviant, knew no limits of compressive force that it would bear, and which rewarded the dutiful compressor with an abundant splash of properly fragranted fluid such that its compressor, if it had any momentary inclination to decompress, would reinstate itself in an even more firm and dignified manner so that the pleasant process could be dutifully renewed.

Park was aghast. Lorenzostein had foisted his faux empathetic personality on R and had won her heart with his self-effacing easiness, obvious desire to raise a family with her, and to some small degree (Perk pardoned his own pun) with his penal proficiency. This same deviant had enslaved the youthful N at the tender age of twenty-three with his gigantic rougous penis, his tit-gnawing mouth, and his false promises of everlasting affection. And now, the deviant-of-deviants had a 50-year old, elegantly attractive, well-bred, highly socially positioned Pinglish woman on whom he was inflicting his sick psychopathological self!

Perk was actually developing the suspicion that

this was all a crock of shit. N was real, he knew that. But were the details of Lorenzostein's relationship with that obvious Viking Goddess real, or were they a figment of his little sick imagination? And all the crap with R about their sexual relationship, and her supposed affairs? Crap too! And now, more crap! Perk suddenly suspected that Lorenzostein had been feeding him purified crap for 13-years. And now more crap about his so-called Pinglish hot-pot!

According to our hero, he had met K when he had spent a sabbatical year at a prestigious university in her country, with which she happened to be affiliated. They were just friends, as he was with many people there. However, several years later he ran into K while he was briefly passing through on the way to the continent, and their relationship began at that time. Lorenzostein described K as an extremely lady-like, attractive, woman of 50-years of age who was very well-connected in the social set around the University and who was a very capable and respected high-level governmental administrator. Lorenzostein seemed to have found a mature intellectual and emotion companion in K, but, as always, he was fixated on the sexual dimension of their relationship which seemed to be blown far out of proportion in its imagined intensity and valency. Our hero claimed that he was beginning to understand that R was a good person, not the surreptitious nymphomaniac that he had made her out to be. But, he maintained that her muted sensuality and their lack of a strong sexual and emotional connection had driven him to an exaggerated state if desperation and despair. His gigantic autonomous penis had a self-directed need to be attended to and cared for, yet his empathetic personality and his commitment to his family life kept him tied to R. The ensuing tension, according to Lorenzostein, led to a situation in which the sexual aspects of his relationships were blown out of proportion. In his view, in the limited amount of time that he spends with his mistresses he seeks to quench his most basic needs and provide himself with a sense of satiety that will carry him through the everyday sexual and emotional blandness of his marriage to the 'good', but not loving in a sexually or emotionally passionate manner, R.

After hearing our friend's pseudo-sincere, semi-insightful discourse on these various subjects, Perk was increasingly convinced that he was dealing with a manipulative, self-deluding, falsely empathetic, woman-hating deviant of the worst kind, who was now in the process of enslaving another lovely member of the gentle sex. Perk recalled a story that Lorenzostein had matter-of-factly told him, early in his treatment, about the very first mistress he had taken after his marriage to R, during the sexual plentitude of the early 1970s. According to the deviant's telling of this bizarre tale, his 'relationship' with this unfortunate married woman involved him tying her to a vertical heating pipe in her kitchen and then frying greasy hamburger meat on the stove nearby for 15-minutes after which he would ravish her while she stood bound to the pipe. After two weeks of this animalistic ritual, our bearded deviant concluded that she had become conditioned to expect ravishing sex after being exposed to the smell of frying hamburger. Thereafter, he cooked the hamburger with the damsel tied to the pipe, but refused to ravish her. As told by Lorenzostein, this mutually-agreed upon conditioning experiment by two brilliant advanced graduate students produced a long-lasting desire by the female participant to have immediate ravishing sex whenever she was exposed to the olfactory sensation of frying hamburger meat, and less intensely when she smelled any other frying or roasting meat. This caused a number of serious problems for the unfortunate young lady as she attempted to cope with university dining facilities, fast food restaurants, and other obstacles to social tranquility during the subsequent ten years or so.

Perk knew the difference between mutual sexual exploration and enslavement. There was no mutuality in Lorenzostein's exuberant sexual thirst! What was reflected in his behavior was a driven and predatory enslavement of lovely dignified ladies like R and K, as well as more robust and luscious lasses like N, by this bearded, wild-eyed, big-dicked predator who went by the unlikely name of Lorenzostein.

There was another aspect of our hero's sexual relationship/exploitation with/of K that gave Perk additional insights into the perverted manner in which he enslaved his female prey. In recounting to Perk the satisfying features of his sexual entanglement with K, Lorenzostein incessantly repeated, in a clearly deranged perseverating manner, his hallucinatory portrayal of what he sensitively described as his favorite copulatory position with K. This entailed the pervert of perverts lying on his back in bed with his supposedly gigantic erect penis pointed skyward (or ceilingward, as was the most frequent, but not only, case). How the erect penis had achieved it splendid state was not made entirely clear, but it appeared that it primarily involved preliminary activities in a vertical position. Apparently, K made the rapid emotional transition from elegant lady to, in Lorenzostein's words, exquisite seductress in response to his removing her upper coverings while he, himself, had already shed his clothes. Then, as he passionately kissed her lovely lips and mouth and breasts, she would gently press her modest, and lady-like, bottom against his increasingly colossal mass while at the same time grasping the inner flanks of his thighs and the root and testicles of the object of her desire -- thereby producing an erection more magnificent than anything ever known in the classical world. According to Lorenzostein, he would then lie on his back on the bed, or ground, as described above, and the elegant K would, straddling his recumbent torso, insert his bulbous tip into her most sacred spot. So mounted upon her magnificent steed, K would proceed to exert her fullest repetitive thrusting forces upon her beloved's hardened staff, while assuming the possessed visage of Saint Joan, herself, riding into battle as her pleasure swelled. Lorenzostein responded to her challenge with his own sharp, projective, retorts, while clenching her buttocks in his frenzied grasp, wishing only that she could somehow have her fingernails more properly embedded in his own rear.

To the good Dr. Perk it was clear many times over that our poor hero was nothing more than a delusional, totally psychotic sexual predator who had developed a deceivingly empathetic personality that led certain innocent women, who may have been denied parental affection or chocolate in their youth, to open themselves to his swirling affections. Given this initial and most innocent emotional/sexual opening, the deviant predator known as Lorenzostein would then enslave his prey with wine and talk and forest creature sex of the type long condemned by the moral authority of the dominant religion and by its highest local representative, Oriole Outlaw. It was this uncontrollable preoccupation with exploitative sex in every phase of his life which made Lorenzostein the complete deviant that he was and a serious menace to social tranquility.

The final disgusting manifestation of Lorenzostein's moral decay was a poem that he showed to Perk which he claimed to have written for K.

AN ODE TO MY MISTRESS' COMPOST HEAP

Most fertile heap
That doth lay down its mass upon the sodden soil.
What brings your warmth up out from down within your central part?
What force of nature doth bestow on thee such incendiary kindle?
That thy sweet surface lies ablaze
Like Pompeii's ruinous flame.

Most delicious grass.
Most fragrant and perfumed of holes
Thy gurgling chime invites my most intemperate plunge
To sink within thy everlasting embrace
And pass eternity in thy soup.

What geologically yellow muds,
With blues and browns and reds all interlaced?

What boiling sauce of former green delight?
What heaven-sent carriage descended to bear
A youthful lad or near spent sir
Up onto his most proper place?

And then,
When hoisted up into the spot
What jellied movements doth this heap begot?
What ecstasy it doth provide
To he who is privileged to ride
Its flaming, moss-bedangled, vessel of beguile.

So, to thee I give my everlasting love.
To plait my strands among your noble straws.
To bear my heart upon thy leafy breast.
To see fermented in this thing
The joyous strings of our life as one.

CHAPTER 10 LORENZOSTEIN'S FURTHER DECLINE

The news was grim for our friend. The senior faculty of the Department of Shitology, the two full Professors, had voted against his request to be promoted from the rank of Associate Professor to that of Professor. Lorenzostein was crushed. The letter of denial, from Red Grant, the most meritorious member of the Department, contrasted Lorenzostein's "academic output" (in terms of numbers of journal articles and books) to that of Red, himself, and faulted Lorenzostein for his lack of academic productivity. They had not even sent out Lorenzostein's publications (scholarship) to be reviewed by competent scholars in his particular area of shitology, nor was there any effort made to assess his scholarly reputation in the field of shitology, which was very high -- higher even than Red's! Nothing was said about the centrality of Lorenzostein's scholarship to the field of shitology, while, in contrast, Red Grant's work, although there was more of it, was concerned with the most mundane and unimportant aspects of shitology and much of this so-called scholarship was published in unrefereed trade magazines, not scholarly journals.

Our hero was stunned by the harshness of this denial. If his scholarship had been reviewed by experts in his field and found lacking, then that would have been a fair review. But, for the small-penised doody wee wees in the third rate Department of Shitology at U-TRASH, none of whom have any expertise in his field of research, to refuse to review him for promotion to the exalted rank of Doody Professor of Wee Wee was clearly a political act rather than a scholarly decision. Lorenzostein was despised at U-TRASH because he was not a member of the dominant religious group and because of his perceived non-traditional lifestyle, which would have been accepted as normal in virtually any part of America except in Trashtown under the watchful eye of Oriole Outlaw and the full force of the dominant religious group. In contrast, President Herpie's many liaisons, and the scandalous affairs of Dean Luogano and Sub-Sub Dean Henry Halfdickless with the notorious Shelley Flame, were not faulted.

Lorenzostein was absolutely devastated by this professional rejection by his academic colleagues in the Department of Shitology and in the Administration at U-TRASH. It was shortly after this unhappy time that Perk, who was now doing little to actively help our unfortunate hero and who was merely charting his decline, began to notice the most profound symptoms of our friend's growing mental distress. One of the first signs of Lorenzostein's transition from agitated mild psychosis to a full-blown florid psychotic personality occurred just at this time, and was apparently precipitated by his crushing professional defeat. This occurred when the increasingly disoriented Lorenzostein reported to Perk about the voices that he had begun to hear in his head. Apparently, Lorenzostein had accompanied R to church one Sunday, which was unusual for him. At this particular service there was a segment devoted to prayers from the assembled for members of the congregation in need. During this segment, a mother addressed the assembly and described the "mental illness" of her teenage daughter, a prominent feature of which was the fact that the girl constantly heard repetitive phrases in her head. Lorenzostein was a bit taken back by the characterization of this as "mental illness," for there were a number of phrases which constantly flowed through his head and which he would verbalize from time to time, either when under stress or when sexually aroused. Hearing the categorization of this behavior as "mental illness" was a wake-up bell to our hero which caused him considerable immediate anxiety. This led him to take communion, which was not his usual practice, perhaps as some sort of preventative or expurgative.

Calmly, Lorenzostein conveyed to Perk how for the past several years he had heard the phrase "Doody wee wee, doody wee wee" racing through his head, usually for two refrains of:

Doody wee wee, Doody wee wee
Doody wee wee, Doody wee wee

and how the occurrence of this refrain in his mind had become more frequent and more emotionally intense in recent weeks. Instead of a dull continuous background sound that would occasionally reach into his consciousness, it had now become a throbbing blare that he frequently verbalized aloud. Our friend had concocted a bizarre pseudo-religious explanation for this demented noise and explained it away as some form of chant that his mind used to block out the evil and hypocritical cant that surrounded him in everyday life. In an even more bizarre manner, the rapidly disintegrating deviant had constructed a completely cockeyed explanatory system for his mental mutterings. According to the recently humiliated shitologist, each individual during their lives, and entire societies, are characterized by a delicate balance between the doody component (which Lorenzostein claimed was bad and repressive) and the wee wee component (which Lorenzostein, in his wisdom, maintained was good and creative) of their lives. In the view that he put forward in these declining months of his life, social life represents a continual conflict between the "doody" and the "wee wee" elements of the human personality. Our shitological hero claimed that he is able to perceive these components in everyday life and weigh them verbally in terms of the relative loudness and emotional intensity that he gives to the "doody" word and the "wee wee" word during his mutterings at any one point in time. He maintained that this does not indicate that he is "mentally ill," but that he is a highly introspective analytical individual who is seeking to understand both his own personality development as well as the overall forces which shape social flow. He maintained that this is achieved through his own self-created, explanatory system, which he contrasted to the explanatory systems that are provided by religion, secular psychiatry, and various social scientific analyses.

Perk smiled broadly as the tall, bearded, wild-eyed Lorenzostein lay subserviently on his couch muttering madly about doody and wee wee. Of course, there are a number of possible explanations for such phenomena, but the possible explanation which the eminent Dr. Perk would choose to make, and he was certain that it was the possible explanation the distinguished Professor Fey Nayward would also favor, is that Lorenzostein is a completely psychotic madman!

Perk became even more secure in his conviction that Lorenzostein was an incorrigible deviant and that the forces of society must extirpate him from their midst. To that end, he conveyed a continuous stream of our poor hero's depraved thoughts, notions, and actions to Fey Nayward who, working directly with Dean Mess Luogano and Sub-Sub Dean Henry Halfdickless at the behest of President Herpie Smerpy, compiled a "Dossier on the Deviancy of Associate Professor Lorenzostein," which was conveyed to Johnny Press, the University Counsel. Perk also sent this damning material directly to the University medical insurance carrier so that it would be entered in Lorenzostein's medical records independently of University sources. Perk felt a certain sanctimonious pleasure in cutting Lorenzostein down to size, so to speak.

Our friend also reported a second repetitive refrain to Perk which he said had been racing through his head for a while, and much more intensely during the past few weeks. This bizarre phrase ran as follows:

Enslaved to a Large-Penised Male

Lorenzostein claimed that this phrase coursed through his mind repetitively, especially when he was sexually aroused, although he also thought it might appear when he was anxious, and he believed that the two refrains might occur in the same general thought process (during, say, a five-minute period of time), but not in immediate juxtaposition to one another. Our friend was certain that this second refrain reflected his attitude toward women in some way, either:

1) That the best male lovers should take the unfettered initiative in seducing women in general, or perhaps a large group of certain chosen women, as these femininely-empathetic males carry the seed of a more gentle, or considerate, society; or

2) That all women, or a large sub-group of the best women, will seek out and choose who they perceive to be the most desirable males and will take these femininely-empathetic males as their long-term lovers, and it is these males who will provide the seed of a more gentle, or considerate, society.

Lorenzostein favored the second explanation for this repetitive refrain and believed that what this represented was a reminder in his mind that it is his social duty to make himself as appealing as possible to women, who will then choose to seduce him. At that time, it is his further duty to sexually and emotionally satisfy those women (enslave them to The Large-Penised Male) who have been so generous as to favor him with their gifts. The first explanation also had some valency for our hero, but only as an admonition that he should always be ready and prepared to respond to female overtures and that it may, at times, be necessary to take some preliminary steps to inflame the reticence of appropriate women. This should be done by making his potential interest crystal clear so as to reduce any anxiety on the part of the member of the fair sex that an initiative which she may take would overstep the bounds of propriety.

To say that Perk's grin was broad would be a gross understatement. Lorenzostein had just sealed his fate. What complete deviancy to be walking around the streets of Trashtown with the expression "Enslaved to a Large-Penised Male" running through one's head, and what further compound deviancy to have these outrageous sociobiological-sounding explanations suggesting that women are seducing certain men and that these men consequently sexually enslave their seductresses. Total deviant perversion! Perk quickly decided that he would not only enter this information in Lorenzostein's psychiatric health insurance provider records and pass them on immediately to Fey Nayward, but that he, Dr. Perk, would step into this moral breach and directly inform Herpie Smerpy, President of U-TRASH at Trashtown, and Hilly Pulver, Thane of the entire multi-campus U-TRASH system, of the total and complete mental and moral depravity of their employee. Furthermore, he, himself, would directly inform Oriole Outlaw of this diabolical deviancy that he has found wandering among his flock and urge the Oriole, in no uncertain terms, to bring the full force of the dominant religious group to bear on this intolerable situation through the Oriole's controlling influence with Thane Pulver and President Herpie. Why should he let Herpie, Luogano, Halfdickless, and Fey get all of the credit and all of the rewards for this, when it is he, Perk, who has done all of the work to extract these confessions of deviancy from the putrid deviant. So what if Lorenzostein had not actually done anything, and so what if Luogano and Halfdickless have been humping the delectable Shelley Flame! Lorenzostein has thoughts in his mind which are clearly deviant. Perk had never heard such preposterous ideas except from among criminally-confined individuals and institutionalized psychotics. Certainly, eminent scholars like Fey Nayward and JB Hawkblack and other contributing members of the Department of Shitology do not walk the corridors of

U-TRASH with such sick thoughts in their minds! Over the days and weeks following his denial of promotion by the Department of Shitology, our most unfortunate hero conveyed to Perk a cascade of repetitive thoughts and psychotic mental perambulations which the good doctor patiently recorded complete with his highly critical analytical commentary. Apparently, our friend had another repetitive sequence that regularly echoed through his consciousness. In some manner that is only accessible to total perverted deviants like Lorenzostein, the large-penised madman had fixated on a bizarre conjugation of what he claimed was a Panish verb. It was the repetitive conjugation of this verb, in the present tense, which he reported to be swirling through his mind.

Erectar - To Erect

Erecto	Erectamos
Erectas	Erectais
Eracta	Erectan

Lorenzostein's inklings about what precipitated these thoughts and what they meant were a further confirmation of his madness. The bearded deviant seemed to think that these repetitive thoughts, which he said that he frequently verbalized as "chants," were some sort of incantations which aided him in warding off his "enemies." According to the overly-penised madman, these phrases, along with the others which he had previously revealed to Dr. Perk, welled up in his head as his "enemies" set upon him in innumerable nefarious ways. He claimed that these repetitive phrases racing through his head helped him to mobilize his energies and cast aside the depression induced in him by his tormentors' constant scorn. Furthermore, Lorenzostein maintained that these very phrases were his way of making fun of his "enemies" to himself. By using these "chants" he reduced their pompous, power- and money-fixated behavior, and their psychopathological ego-protective cruelty and complete hypocrisy, to a concrete and ironically humorous level. Again, Perk nodded politely as he reviewed with Lorenzostein the details of what he had just said, while at the same time salivating modestly at the thought of how he would incorporate this completely illogical nutcrap into his report to President Herpie and his prominence, Oriole Outlaw.

The final suite of crazed ideas rattling around in our friend's head, which he conveyed to Perk, were not repetitive phrases, but a grandiose scenario which he said had been slowly growing in his mind. The theme of this millennial fantasy was that Lorenzostein, who now usually called himself The Large-Penised Male, viewed himself as some semi-religious savior who had come to Earth from outer space in order to establish a new Kingdom of Considerate Civility and Deep Personal Empathy among all humans. In order to establish this kingdom, The Large-Penised Male had been sent to Earth to copulate with the greatest possible number of the most physically, emotionally, and socially appropriate female humans so that he would directly convey to them his precious ZNA -- the vehicle, designed by the Principal Investigator in outer space, for transmitting Lorenzostein's empathetic personality to the population in future generations, who would then form the basis of his new Kingdom. Also, in order to further hasten the arrival of this new day, the Large-Penised Male and his growing gaggle of large, medium, and small-titted disciples would go about dispersing large amounts of His Preciousness's fresh rich semen into the air and into the communal water supplies of cities, towns, and villages worldwide so that the future fruit of this new kingdom would be most bounteous.

And most importantly, His Preciousness had decreed July 6th of each year as "Tush Day," a time when all peoples of the Earth will be given the opportunity to sit down simultaneously and renew their lifelong commitment to His Preciousness. For on this day they will gain entrance to his Kingdom by making their largest possible contribution to Lorenzostein. This could be done most simply by sitting on their home throne, or from publically available thrones. In his increasingly disconnected manner, Lorenzo carefully explained to Perk how he, Lorenzostein, The Large-Penised Male, and his disciples would make their own exemplary contributions at exactly 12 noon Lorenzoland time, which is the same time as Pashington, P.C. time. Lorenzostein, speaking in this same relaxed manner that was devoid of his usual wild-eyed mania, calmly maintained that the President of the Pnited Ptates, G. T. Tush, his right-hand person, D. Chainsaw, and his left-hand person, Gin Rummy, had agreed to take their places on unenclosed public thrones on the Phite Pouse lawn and would be ready to go at 12 noon. Having just been denied promotion to full Professor, our hero told Perk that he had decided that he should leave the abusive public sector environment of the Department of Shitology at U-TRASH and attempt to make a go of it in the private sector by making Lorenzoland, his new Kingdom of Considerate Civility and Deep Personal Empathy, his life's work and the manifestation of his new commitment to entrepreneurship and the market economy.

Lorenzostein then related the following plan to Perk in the most even-tempered and sincere manner. In order to develop Lorenzoland as an integrating institution for all peoples, he would request that the inhabitants of planet Earth all make gifts in money to him, Lorenzostein, on a regular basis. He related to Perk the different gift levels and the appellations that a person would be entitled to with each of these various levels of gifting:

$25 annually	Ordinary Giver
$50 annually	Extraordinary Giver
$100 annually	Splendid Giver
$500 annually	Plentiferous Giver
$1,000 annually	Tush Level Giver
$5,000 annually	Puffet Level Giver
$10,000+	Still Plates Level

Lorenzostein told Perk that if he receives many gifts it will hopefully enable him to leave the drudgery of shitology behind and, instead, build himself a vast castle and create Lorenzoland and commence living a life of elegance comparable to that of Still Plates. He would then proceed to turn Lorenzoland, his new Kingdom of Considerate Civility and Deep Personal Empathy, into an agency for social good on a worldwide basis.

Perk had stopped taking notes about half-way through Lorenzostein's self-absorbed psychotic ruminations about Tush Day and Lorenzoland. He just sat back and looked down at the tall, bearded pervert obediently lying on his couch and wondered whether at this advanced stage of his psychosis he was even able to get an erection. Even if he could get an erection, Perk doubted that he would know what to do with it at this point. He would probably try to stick it into the water meter! The delusional, sex-fixated, messianic themes of these heretical thoughts would surely be of interest to his prominence, Oriole Outlaw, who will undoubtedly bring the full force of the dominant religious group down on Lorenzostein. Perk had heard directly from President Herpie that Oriole Outlaw and Thane Hilly Pulver had predominant authority in dealing with matters of religious orthodoxy in Trashtown, and that the Thane's criminal brother, Blackie Pulver, would be used to put the clamps on the deviant Lorenzostein in the very place that would make him somewhat less, or very much less, than a large-penised male. Lorenzostein's days were clearly numbered, and Perk looked forward with relish to the moment when he would finally learn that Lorenzostein, so to speak, had gone back to outer space.

CHAPTER 11 THE DEMISE OF PERK

As Lorenzostein entered this period of rapid mental decline Perk began to suspect the bearded deviant, despite his apparent disorientation, was fiddling with a young patient of his by the name of Lotte Stacken. Lotte was a 16-year-old child who was just in the process of maturing into a voluptuous woman. Actually, she had been a voluptuous woman for at least a year, and was having great difficulty reconciling the moral teachings of her home and church with the increasingly volcanic yearnings of her flesh. Both her first and her last names were uniquely descriptive of this budding maiden and Perk felt privileged to have been entrusted with her therapy and mentoring by her very socially-prominent parents. However, on a recent occasion (in the ten-minute period after Lorenzostein's appointment and before Lotte's, when Perk usually completed his notes on his session with the deviant) Perk left his office early, a few minutes after our hero's departure, and was appalled to hear raucous sounds of what he believed to be copulatory delight coming from the locked ladies room outside of his office. Perk's extremely discreet and incredulous inquiry was answered by Lotte in a firm and reassuring voice whose articulation seemed to falter, as though a large firm object had been inserted to the level of her vocal chords, or, as though some mud-like substance had suddenly encaked her speech apparatus. Perk was certain that Lorenzostein was in the washroom with Lotte, and that he had caught the deviant inflicting his animalistic needs on her pure, but vulnerable, flesh.

From that fateful day forward, Perk, with his mentation increasingly agitated, began to see Lotte not as a youthful innocent who had been entrusted to his paternalistic care, but as a gift from the gods, an exquisite sample of budding womanhood. This divine-sent offering was his reward for a life of pious rectitude. Moreover, he began to see it as his sacred duty to initiate this extremely full-bodied near-vestal being into the world of emotional and physical maturity so that she would acquire a healthy attitude toward the proper role of the woman as caring and compliant wife. Yes, Perk concluded with his characteristic incisiveness. It is an issue of modesty and restraint bordering on passivity! The problem lay not with the uncontrollable sexual exuberance of the female which can be sated only by the carnal lust of deviant males like Lorenzostein, but, it is a question of the proper social shaping of natural womanly enthusiasms. This molding of the budding female psyche requires that they be given proper direction under the firm hand and authoritative guidance of established leaders and pillars of society, and that they be shielded at all costs from the dissipated debauchery of the deviant dregs who wander the streets with their long dripping pipes.

It became clear to Perk, crystal clear, clear as night is distinguished from day, that these young flowers of our social patch must be taken and initiated by the forces of good to protect them from the creeping forces of evil that lurk in every corner. That Lotte was sent to him, the estimable Dr. Perk, not to the deviant Lorenzostein! That it is his absolute social duty to take her and empty into her, and for her to thus learn the joys of obedience under the subjugation of his ruling thing. And, said the good doctor to himself repeatedly, his thing is quite sufficient to the task, just ask Mrs. Perk!

Influenced by the growing awareness of his just-realized social obligation, Perk commenced a period of frenzied planning and anticipation of the moment that he would pounce on the recumbent maiden and fully reveal himself to her in all of his accomplished majesty. The reserved, authoritative, aging Dr. Perk had become obsessed by Lorenzostein's lurid tales of sexual predation and now viewed the large-breasted, amply-assed Lotte lying on his therapeutic couch from his analytical seat, with his fully erect, but miniscule, thing extending down his trouser as far as its minisculeness would take it, and with his trouser leg slightly damp from its miniscule premature effort. Lorenzostein always stuck his tongue deeply into their mouths and then went directly for their nipples, first through their clothing and then in the flesh immediately after that rude encasement had been ripped asunder. After these momentary preliminaries he would enter them forcefully or gently, depending on the case. Perk would do the same! He had heard it a million times. And, he had even engaged in some modest fantasizing about the lovely Lotte complete with left handed masturbation just to make it more realistic. Clean, healthy normal maritally-focused genital sex is what they must be taught and not the wild-eyed, multi-orifice, buttocks slapping, sledge hammer-like depravity of Lorenzostein and his deviant ilk.

Thus, on an otherwise uneventful day in the month of February in the year 1998, as Lotte Stacken lay on the eminent Dr. Perk's analytic couch immobilized by the uncertainty of her relative affections for the young actors Natt Ramon and Carlo Leonardo, the eminent doctor, in the sixty-third year of his life, raised himself out of his therapeutic seat and, as though he was possessed by the very body of the depraved Lorenzostein, threw himself atop the terrified lass and commenced to engage in, or attempted to engage in, what was charitably described in the press as a "deviant carnal act."

CHAPTER 12 A NECESSARY PAUSE

As a consequence of Perk's arrest, imprisonment, mental breakdown, and treatment with electroshock therapy, the main source of impartial descriptive data on Lorenzostein and his nefarious ways has been, for the moment, hidden from our view. Our hero's mental collapse and hospitalization after losing access to his beloved therapist has made it even more difficult to chart his continuing saga. Perk's likely release from prison in the not-too-distant future, Lorenzostein's remarkable response to his aggressive treatment with dilute solutions of organic fava beans, and the Principal Investigator's apparent success in tinkering with aspects of Lorenzostein's programming, and with his antenna itself, gives us some hope that our needed data will soon begin to flow and that our story will further unfurl in the foreseeable future.

The outcomes of the continuing battles between Lorenzostein and his small penised doody wee wee adversaries is certainly of great interest to all of humankind as is the question of Lorenzostein's success in establishing Lorenzoland and his Kingdom of Considerate Civility and Deep Personal Empathy. Whether our hero will actually be able to have Tush Day, on July 6th, accepted as a national holiday in the Pnited Ptates is another question of universal interest.

The future reader is also likely to be intrigued with the Principal Investigator's new research focus on the social uses of deviancy in Pamerican society, using his thick analyses of JB Hawkblack's varied career as a case study. These thrilling episodes shall be forthcoming following Perk's eventual release and Lorenzostein's hoped for recovery. .

EPILOGUE: LORENZOSTEIN'S UNFINISHED CANTOS

These passages, which were found among Lorenzostein's papers after his collapse, seem to represent cantos from an unfinished poetical effort on his part. We present them below without comment.

THE SLEEP OF BABES

It was perhaps 5 AM and the sun was just rising above the horizon and entering an agnathous sky laced with an emerald hue reminiscent of Olbian shores. Lorenzostein lay in his customary place near the edge of his double bed with R on the other side, near her edge, and with the covers and blankets mounded up between them like some sort of purposeful barrier. Lorenzostein actually lay on his back and through the thick haze of his awakening condition could feel the fullness of his mighty sword as it slowly made its way to begin its journey toward the light. He could feel his covers tent up above its arching aspect as the visual picture of K, clad in the full armor of Saint Joan with hair cropped short and mounted on her steed, came wafting through his consciousness, as his possessed mistress decisively thrust upon his exuberant fullness with the ecstasy of full orgasm on her face. Perhaps his mouth became a bit moist as he lumbered back to sleep pursued by vaguer images of yet unknown, but likely to be known, soft-mouthed, large-breasted ladies whose comely visages had recently graced his view. He knew that they would make the first gesture, and he knew that it was his sacred duty to relieve them of the discomfort of initiating any further advance.

Hawkblack stirred quietly as the events of the previous day coursed through his little wee wee. He had been very courtly with Pivion and he had squired her to several public events where they had been seen together, thus reinforcing his identification as being sexually standard. Of course, he couldn't stay with her overnight because he had to fly off later in the evening on a top secret 0-0-HAWKBLACK mission to save the free world from the clutches of some unknown Uznonesuchstani tribal leader. The Agency, based on surveillance information from 0-0-HAWKBLACK, suspected that Lorenzostein was a secret agent for this extremist despot and they had decided, on 0-0-HAWKBLACK'S urging, to greatly expand their surveillance and counter-espionage efforts against him. This morning, 0-0-HAWKBLACK and Jymboloso, his companion in this appropriate use of the taxpayers' money, were flying a cargo of a new type of high explosive plastique that Jymboloso had developed down to intelligence headquarters in Pangly to test it out for possible use against the extremist Lorenzostein. While in Pangly they would make sure to stop in at the conveniently nearby "Young Lads Disco" to catch both the 8 PM and 10 PM "14 and Under" show, as

Hawkblack had finally gotten a date with Arnold, the delectably submissive young blond lead dancer. JB's wee wee resonated with excitement about what would transpire with the much-coveted Arnold, and what would soon happen to that extremist deviant Lorenzostein.

Beneath an emerald sky that could only be called agnathous, Fey Nayward turned in his bed to face the sacred direction as he commenced the early morning ritual component of his devotion to his most-beloved, and quite accommodating, Herman. The very decent Mrs. Nayward was safely ensconced in her own bedroom, an arrangement foisted on their very proper "marriage" long ago by the Fagster in a garbled tirade about work, and energy, and rest, and of the importance of restraint, and of high moral values. In his morning observance, as in his more frenzied evening session just before bed, Fey would hang a life-sized picture of the youthful, blond and unadorned Herman on the wall so that it was facing in the precise direction of Herman's overcushioned apartment, where the blond bombshellet was kept by the Fagster and several high-end, and equally dignified, bon vivants at U-TRASH -- one of whom has been mentioned above. With Herman Belvedere securely established in his temple, Fey would attempt to boot up his "little pink" as delectable visual images of the delightful one danced through his dark mind and into his diminutive dick. In the midst of his moaning and drooling Fey's pleasure was drawn to an abrupt conclusion on this particular day (as it had been much too often recently) by a rather firm knock on his door -- some would even say a harsh bang -- and the voice of the earnest-sounding Mrs. Nayward inquiring whether she had left the condoms in his room -- despite the fact that Fey and his symbol of propriety had not had sex for years.

Under that same agnathous emerald sky, Red Grant lay in his bed in the room next to Mrs. Grant. The early swirl of dawn was just crossing his eyes as he recalculated his total assets accounting for yesterday's rise in the stock market. He had forgotten to include that day's increase in the value of his smaller IRA accounts and the appreciation in value of his house over the past week when he had run the numbers through his head five minutes ago. Red was the self-described 'most meritorious' member of the Department of Shitology and he basked like a hippopotamus in the warm mud-like glow of his financial success. His salary was fifty percent greater than Lorenzostein's! And well it should be, for he, Red, had turned out eight short articles in trolley car and brake person trade magazines this year as well as eleven book reviews in the same publications, each at least two hundred words in length. Furthermore, he had been a featured speaker at the prestigious Monthly Meeting of the Central Pasian Trolley Car and Brakeperson Association in Exile at Camden, New Somewhere. And the goddam passive jerks in Shitology had not even questioned him on this one and had given him frumpteen merit points, thanks to Shenzi's able chairpersonship of the Shitology Merit Committee this year -- an effort that will definitely hasten Shenzi's departure from the bottom of the pile in Shitology. And the deviant Lorenzostein had been given fewer merit points for his well-received scholarly volume on *Biological and Cultural Adaptation to*

This and That. Under Red's watchful eye, the hand-flapping Fey had extracted volumes of confidential psychiatric information from the doltish Dr. Perk, and Hawkblack, under Red's executive guidance, was preparing a pleasant little gift for the bearded deviant. President Herpie had promised the Department of Shitology that they would receive triple the normal amount of merit monies when they finally send Lorenzostein back to outer space, and Red was placing himself in a position to assure that he, not those little assholes in Shitology, would receive most of it. Red Grant was content. However, he had noticed, without concern, that while he spent so much time plotting against Lorenzostein, his wife, Mrs. Grant, was spending a considerable amount of time in the company of his recently retired stockbroker neighbor, Mr. Dick.

Under a sky that has been clearly described above, Buck Schmuckperson slept flat on his back in a position similar to that of military attention, although it was somewhat more glorious, given Schmuckperson's overall leaderly perfectness and his complete moral purity honed over the years in the course of his extensive travels through the prominent religious and cultural fads of the time. In order to further enhance his moral purity and beat back any sensual passions which might possibly arise in his leaderly loins, Buck had constructed a device which continuously sprayed cold water over his sleeping form, with its epicenter of coldness focused on his "little pistol," as he preferred to call his private part. Mrs. Schmuckperson was housed in separate quarters, so to speak, a concession the leaderly one made to her need for Pordic solitude and, perhaps, because she preferred to sleep in a dry bed away from the constant spill of pompous babble that gushed from the All-Knowing Schmuck. Schmuckperson always kept his "little pistol" in his holster, perhaps another reason why his wife preferred to sleep alone. At this early hour he frequently thought of Lorenzostein and his perverted deviancy, and with the first light of day crawling beneath his lids he cringed in contempt of the tall, bearded, wild-eyed, Pewish deviant who he, himself, was personally committed to hounding and humiliating into complete sexual impotence and total marginalization within U-TRASH. After Lorenzostein is destroyed he, Schmuckperson, would be more than willing to take over the mentoring, advising in the terms used by the University, of some of the tasty-looking female snatch that the deviant had wilely accumulated among his student advisees. In the dimness of the morning, Schmuckperson felt a momentary twiggle in his pistol and, with a hand guided by his devotion to innumerable passing cults, deftly turned the faucet from cold to freezing.

The rising lightness of the day was complemented by the lightness of Vladimir Haverford's near-empty head as it, and he, rolled from side to side gasping, with an excruciating acclamation of absolute need, "Red! Red!" and then, snorting and gobbling as he, in his stupor, imagined that he had finally inserted his head between Red's ample cushions, and in the utter safety of that place could ply his trade in his expert way. He would rail against Lorenzostein for the bearded one's supposedly wanton ways with his practiced sanctimoniousness, and he would suck up to Red by lauding his extraordinary scholarly productivity and smart Barry's Poystown attire. He, Vladimir Haverford, had recently been a Distinguished Visiting Halfbright Scholar at an foreign university, and if he played his cards right and kept his head to the grindstone, so to speak, he might someday make it to Distinguished Visiting Allbright Scholar, and then even, he could barely tolerate the excitement that it brought to his near-empty mind, with Red's full-bodied support he hoped to be promoted to Doody Professor of Wee Wee! Vladimir's miniscule thing tingled and sizzled with delight as in the foggy hours of the morn he wondered who N, that long-lost but not forgotten large-titted and amply assed Viking Goddess at U-TRASH, would now prefer -- the hounded, marginalized, near-shaking and muttering deviant Lorenzostein, or the present Distinguished Visiting Halfbright Professor who, despite his obvious limitations, was clever enough to stay well off the bottom of the pile in Shitology.

Perk did not sleep well in the county jail. He had learned that the hard way, so to speak, his first night in The House, but had quickly feigned a heart attack and had been transferred to the medical unit. His attorney had told him that if he could fake a convincing prolonged psychotic break that he could probably get him moved to the psychiatric unit and that with time off for good behavior he might be out in just over five years. Perk had telephoned Fey Nayward and President Herpie incessantly, but they did not respond to his pleas. What bothered him most was why he, the eminent Dr. Perk, was so compromised, while the large-penised deviant Lorenzostein, who did it four or five times a day, often with different women, and frequently in public places, was free. And Fey Nayward, he is a closeted buffy-haired fruitball and an exploiter of young boys! And JB Hawkblack, he is an institutionalizable militaristic psychopath of the totally delusional variety. Nevertheless, he smiled with a certain contentment knowing that he had acted in an open and honorable way and, judging from Lotte's oft-remembered squeals, he firmly believed that he had done his duty. Although he was no longer able to have even his flaccid little erections because of the electroshock treatment, Perk luxuriated in his thought of his moment of eternal glory uncaring about what the future might bring.

On that same morning under that same notable sky, Herpie Smerpy lay in her own twin bed in the same room as Mr. Herpie. She did not worry much about Lorenzostein, as that responsibility had been delegated to Mess Luogano and Henry Halfdickless, for which they were amply rewarded. Herpie always awoke at the crock of dawn, so to speak, so that she could quickly leave her sacred marital abode for her early morning spiritual journey with Mess and her noon to 3 PM working lunch with Thane Hilly Pulver in his multi-couched suite of rooms in his enormous office on Break-in Hill. Hilly didn't have much to work with, but he had a certain boyish enthusiasm for her modestly-large-for-her-size breasts. And Hilly didn't fart all over her like Mess! Furthermore, she had never previously, as a condition of employment, been required to have sex with a criminal like Blackie, Hilly's brother. That was a first for her, something to tell her grandchildren about, although most of the other gentlemen at or near the top of academia were not any more good or noble or pure or honest than Hilly and Blackie. At times, when it crossed her mind, Herpie thought that it probably would have been nice to have Lorenzostein as a lover, but he had just not ponied up to her and at some point he became too conspicuous and independent of thought to be allowed to survive at U-TRASH without her patronage -- too much of a threat to her court, she had concluded, and to her two little herps.

The early morning light shined meekly on Mess Luogano, the larger and the louder of the two little herps. This delightful morning found him entwined in the arms of the voluptuous and ambitious Shelley Flame, far from his conjugal bed that he had recently abandoned, after many years of marriage, for the greater moral purity of an academic affair. Other mornings would find him in the equally ambitious arms of Tracy Triber, a member of the Humanities faculty at U-TRASH who was even more solidly constructed than the estimable Flame. Mess had been Herpie's long-term lover, although now they did not bother with one another, and he had every possible bit of dirt on her. One letter by him to the Potlight Team at the Trashtown Orbit and Herpie Smerpy would be sun dried tomatoes! Mess had his own special type of passive aggressive behavior, and as he lay in bed close to the siege of dawn, next to the constantly clawing and pawing Ms. Flame, he quickly rose to enter the bathroom as he felt that very special desire arising at a not particularly socially useful time. For, Mess's special form of entertainment was really his way of constantly reminding Herpie that she was dead meat in his hands, and that he wasn't even going to make his monetary demands explicit. This pleasant little ritual was enacted between them on a regular basis when Mess felt that his salary was rising less rapidly than his galloping expectations. At this time, on the way to lunch, Mess would guide Herpie to the rear elevator in the Administration Building and, using a special code which he entered into the floor selection panel, cause the elevator containing the two senior administrators at U-TRASH to ascend at an extraordinarily slow pace. During their prolonged isolation of approximately 4.87 minutes, Mess would cheerily chat about the most mundane things while he simultaneously loosened volumes of the most fetid fumes upon the entrapped Herpie. Herpie, for her part, endured this indignity without the slightest break in the cadence of her cheery chatter or broad grin, and without even absorbing the conspicuous lacrimation that cascaded down upon her blue dress. Herpie had entrusted Mess with the ultimate responsibility for the full range of illegal and criminal activities to be employed in ridding U-TRASH, and her, of Lorenzostein, and now she had become a prisoner of her own excesses.

As the emerald hue spread further in the agnathous sky Henry Halfdickless, the lesser of the two herps, lay in his conjugal bed next to his beloved wife with thoughts of Shelley's flame lodged prominently in his mind. More prominent, however, were the delightful recollections of the pleasures of the previous day in which he and Mess had carried out a number of highly illegal activities against Lorenzostein at the behest of the many criminals who controlled the Administration at U-TRASH. Like both Herpie and Mess, Halfdickless had very little or no scholarly reputation, but had made his way in academia by slogging through one minor administrative post after another so that after thirty years at U-TRASH, and despite the fact that his academic rank was only that of Associate Professor of Doody, he had waddled his way up into the higher echelons of the Administration. His path to this enviable success was smoothed by the fact that he was a member of the dominant religious group, like all of the other high level administrators, and because he was willing to carry out the dirtiest of Herpie's dirty work with a reserved dignity that was worthy of The Fagster. Actually, he was the main operative, directly under Herpie and Mess, in dealing with the problem of Lorenzostein on a day-to-day basis, and it was through him that 0-0-HAWKBLACK's tapping of Lorenzostein's university telephones were carried out, as were certain entrapment attempts with tasty female 'students' both at U-TRASH and off campus. At times, Halfdickless wondered what he was doing with his life and, as an historian, he saw a glimmer of the similarity between the rise of Pazism in Permany during the 1930s and the way Lorenzostein was being treated at U-TRASH. But the monetary rewards were so ample and Lorenzostein was, thanks to the years-long efforts by the distinguished shitologists, so totally isolated that anyone could say anything about him and it would be considered credible. Anyway, the tall, bearded deviant looked weird and was just different than everyone else. Besides, torturing Lorenzostein was fun and created great camaraderie with some of the best people, his type of people, on campus.

CONCLUSION

And so we have faithfully conveyed to you, the reader, the bizarre tale of the deviant young academic Lorenzostein. We hope that this fable, which is totally and completely fictitious in all of its parts and aspects, has been entertaining to you in the way all fables are meant to entertain, and that whatever parts have caused you to ponder their deeper meanings, or real-life significance, will soon be subordinated to your more worthy pleasures. We must, however, take this opportunity to apologize to you, the reader, for conveying to you, at Lorenzostein's insistence, his bizarre vision of Lorenzoland, his Kingdom of Considerate Civility and Deep Personal Empathy, and of Tush Day and his appeal to the peoples of the world to send him gifts of money periodically. These funds will help Lorenzostein to establish Lorenzoland as a refuge from the abuse he has suffered in the Department of Shitology at U-TRASH, and to live there in the lap of luxury while spreading his precious ZNA-laden seed via his patented spreader. From this secure perch in Lorenzoland, and with your financial support, His Preciousness will be able to combat the perversity, greed and hypocrisy of JB Hawkblack, Fey, Red, Vladimir, Tush and their assorted small-penised, doody wee wee acolytes, and advocate for the downtrodden while working tirelessly for the creation of a Kingdom of Considerate Civility and Deep Personal Empathy that will extend throughout the world.

This is the way that we have heard this bizarre tale, and we feel that it was our responsibility to convey it to you, the reader, so that you may assess its merits as you see fit.

ABOUT THE AUTHOR

Mary Smetley was an academic in several universities in the northeast for a number of years. Since leaving academia she has been living in rural New England doing subsistence agriculture, weaving and pottery as well as turning her hand to writing and poetry.

Printed in Great Britain
by Amazon

56223743R00083